The Sister

A NOVEL OF EMILY DICKINSON

Paola Kaufmann

ROOKERY

OVERLOOK/ROOKERY
NEW YORK, NEW YORK

THE SISTER

This edition first published in The United States of America in 2007 by
The Rookery Press, Tracy Carns Ltd.
in association with The Overlook Press
141 Wooster Street
New York, NY 10012
www.therookerypress.com

This is a work of fiction. Names, characters, places, and incidents are either the product of the author's imagination or are used fictitiously, and any resemblance to actual persons, living or dead, business establishments, events, or locales is entirely coincidental.

Cataloging-in-Publication Data is on file at the Library of Congress

Printed in the United States of America
FIRST EDITION

ISBN 1-58567-951-8
ISBN 13 978-1-58567-951-5

9 8 7 6 5 4 3 2 1

AUTHOR'S NOTE: To write this work of fiction it was necessary to recreate the most important biographical facts, personalities, thoughts, and feelings of the characters of this story, particularly Lavinia and Emily Dickinson. This would not have been possible without consulting certain key texts (biographies, letters, compilations of poems, critical essays) concerning Emily Dickinson, some of which must be mentioned:

Ancestors' Brocades: The Literary Debut of Emily Dickinson (Millicent Todd Bingham); *Austin and Mabel: The Amherst Affair & Love Letters of Austin Dickinson and Mabel Loomis Todd* (Polly Longsworth); *The Belle of Amherst* (William Luce); *Emily Dickinson* (Cynthia Griffin Wolff); *The Hidden Life of Emily Dickinson* (John Evangelist Walsh); *Emily Dickinson's Home: The Early Years as Revealed in Family Correspondence and Reminiscences* (Millicent Todd Bingham); *Emily Dickinson Face to Face: Unpublished Letters, with Notes and Reminiscences* (Martha Dickinson Bianchi); *The Years and Hours of Emily Dickinson* (Jay Leyda); *My Wars Are Laid Away in Books: The Life of Emily Dickinson* (Alfred Habegger); *Emily Dickinson, Crónica de Plata* (*Poemas escogidos*. Selected and translated into Spanish by Manuel Villar Raso).

To all of these above authors, and to the libraries of Smith College, Amherst College, Forbes (Northampton), Jones (Amherst) and the Univerity of Massachusetts, I owe thanks for having been able to write this novel.

—Paola Kaufmann

Prologue

Amherst, Massachusetts, May 1896

*N*obody has ever expected me to write.

In fact, nobody has ever expected anything in particular of me.

With Austin, for example, order was expected. Austin was the law, and that was what was expected from him. Emilie,[1] on the other hand, had to think. She was the only one in this family of proud and self-sufficient monarchs to have the noble duty of *thinking*.

Maybe it was I who should have married. Maybe I was the one destined to have bastard children or to die young – I don't know. The only thing I am certain of is that starting to write at this stage of my life seems presumptuous. It appears that we old folk, as the hour to pack our bags fast approaches, feel almost without exception that we have something important to say.

God knows that I would love to be able to say important

---

1 Throughout her memoirs, Lavinia Dickinson refers to her sister as either "Emilie" or "Emily". The spelling as "Emilie" comes from an affectionate way of calling her from youth, and her own equivalent was "Vinnie", which is how everyone addressed Lavinia. However, Lavinia explicitly chose to continue with this nickname, while Emily Dickinson stopped signing herself as "Emilie" at some stage in her twenties. Although at first Lavinia uses the name in a fairly arbitrary way, it's important to note that Emilie appears in a different, more affectionate light. Emilie is "her sister", while Emily seems to refer more to the poet and to Emily Dickinson as the character who broke free from the limitations of the family house and of the feelings of Lavinia. (Author's note.)

things. Simple things, truths, memories that make no sense to anyone, reflections that do not necessarily fit into my own story – the story of my family.

And yet, ever since my brother Austin died, the only thing that I've done is to blow the dust off papers. Bundles of papers tied together that have lain hidden away and forgotten in trunks, in drawers, in tiny hideaways within neglected furniture in the dark corners and attics of this house, dusty nooks that for years have smelt of old wood; or, to be more precise, have smelt that way since Emilie died, since that afternoon some time after her funeral.

And that was how I also found these old diaries of mine from when I was an adolescent. What courage! But more importantly what simple-mindedness of youth. Now they appear to me both charming and naive, like bunches of lilies in summer. They also seem to me to have been written by somebody else, somebody not me – or perhaps they were written by that somebody that I once was. When someone rediscovers themselves at the bottom of a musty trunk buried in a hidden loft, they find that all was of a different nature, that they felt in a different way, or that maybe there had actually been a different feeling to life itself.

Papers here and there, more papers from Ipswich, from home. Letters. Diaries.[2]

---

2 The Ipswich Diaries, named after the college, Ipswich Female Seminary, that Lavinia Dickinson attended between 1851 and 1852, were destroyed in a flood in the basement of the Evergreens, the house where Austin Dickinson (Emily and Lavinia's elder brother) lived with his own family. The house remains part of the Dickinson Museum. It is said in Amherst that Martha Dickinson, daughter of Austin and the last surviving member of the Dickinsons, saved the Ipswich Diaries of her aunt Lavinia without ever bringing herself to burn them, despite her aunt's expressed request that she do so. Fate made the decision for her: in 1938, almost thirty-nine years after the death of Lavinia Dickinson, a storm of historic magnitude, aided by the ruinous condition of the Evergreens, caused the total flooding of the basement. Of what was there, nothing could be rescued. (Author's note.)

Part One

1

Memories of the Brick House

...There is no such thing as *forgetting* possible to the mind; a thousand accidents may and will interpose a veil between our present consciousness and the secret inscriptions on the mind. Accidents of the same sort will also rend away this veil; but alike, whether veiled or unveiled, the inscription remains for ever.

– T. De Quincey

I

*T*en years, and still these legs can carry me to the cemetery.

I brought lilies of the valley this time. Other people have also remembered – have you noticed? It's covered in flowers! Flowers cover everything. April showers bring May flowers. The magnolia at home, if you could see it, seems clothed in white like a blushing bride. I stare and stare at it as if you were there with me. So close.

But you're here. Everyone is here now. It's not even a year since Austin left me, in August I'll return to bring more flowers. God! How shameful that funeral. How shameful.

It no longer matters. Why tell you about the shame of it if you knew it anyway? Of course you knew about it, only that it was Austin, and as always he was forgiven everything. We weren't forgiven. Perhaps your poetry will save you, but as for me... I've nothing left. All I have left are the dead, the papers, the letters and my pussy cats; and the faithful Maggie who is still going strong, her Irish blood holding her up, like the roots of a cedar supporting the massive trunk through the summer and winter. Through the snow and the wind Maggie keeps going, performing the domestic chores – those things I can no longer perform.

Ten years is a long time, Emilie. In the cemetery the passing of years goes unnoticed; the grass in summer is always green and cut short, the wild flowers come and go, the gravestones proclaim those who lie beneath them. New stones appear bearing new names, but aside from this small detail the cemetery remains the same. Is that not strange? It only changes in winter, when the stones are forgotten beneath the snow, and anyone not knowing where to look would be unable to guess how many dead lie beneath such a small amount of earth.

It's not the same in the town. Our dear Amherst has many hundred more souls than when we buried you, but for some strange reason it's us – the old folk – who make the difference. God insists in taking fresh, young blood. Can you explain to me such a mystery? What can Heaven or Hell possibly do with a soul that is scarcely more than a seed, a heart that neither suffered nor caused anyone to suffer? Is it perhaps the Devil who is nourished on such souls, Emilie? Or is it that we old folk who cling on to life are to be cursed as usurpers for doing so – cursed for claiming as ours that life which, legitimately, belongs to others?

I'm old. Nobody, not even Maggie, should pay any heed to me.

I've now been doing nothing but unearthing these papers for ten years. Or burning them, as you asked me to do thousands of times; and now it seems that I've committed the worst of heresies. I still remember so clearly the afternoon that I opened the old secretaire that nobody had touched since last you touched it, not Maggie while cleaning, nor even me. It had only been a couple of months since your departure, Emilie. It was July, and although in

Amherst, out there beyond the windows, the summer sun beat down, I could scarcely bring myself to approach the darkest corners of the house. I couldn't stop seeing you out of the corner of my eye, seeing you pass silently, wrapped in the scent of musk, ginger and cinnamon that would follow you just like that horrible dog that you so loved would follow you. And the dusting of flour on your dress and on the floor, and the books that you left on the way to your room – that same room that I swear to God I could not enter until two months after you were buried. Was it the pain that it caused me? Too much pain, true, but it's not just that. There was also a powerful fear – do you remember how you used to say that I could recognize things through instinct? But what was I afraid of discovering? That you were no longer there? No, that's not it, I'm not that type of person, I have always known that the dead disappear, and anyway, I can say it now, sometimes I've even wondered whether the dead are not merely fodder for the soil. No, I was frightened of finding you. I was frightened of what you might have left behind, the mercilessness of your writings that were, in essence, your voice.

I've not been good enough, and yet I know, I'm certain, that I've given my entire life to looking after you, to looking after them, and to keeping this house as our own paradise. Bitterness and guilt now take turns to colour my memories. I remember that July afternoon when I asked Maggie to help me clean your room, and she looked at me with a severity that I'd never seen before in her eyes.

"Miss Emily will suffer," she said.

"So will I," I replied. "Let's do it once and for all."

Of course Maggie didn't want to go up there with me. There's no way you can change someone of Irish blood; they would rather die than accept another's bidding. I went alone, with Quincey and Baboo sneaking in beneath my feet, curious and inquisitive – Emilie I swear I wanted to chase them out of your room – you yourself said that the ideal cat is either bearing a great rat in its mouth or not existing in the first place – but I simply couldn't. Carlo, that spoilt mongrel, would gladly have accompanied me had he been alive, so instead I allowed my pussy cats to be the ones to speak to your ghost.

No sooner had they entered than they pressed up close to me, with their eyes fixed on your desk so rigidly that I almost felt I could see you sitting there, writing with your back to the door just as always, your hair done up in a red hairnet, Mother's violet shawl around your shoulders, and your flighty hand, always thin and nervous and stained with ink, dancing above the papers.

Your room had been closed and it smelt of damp, and I reproached myself for having waited so long in going in there. Perhaps it was that need for cleanliness that still governs me now as an old woman that made me forget my fears and, in a fit of passion, run in there and throw open the curtains and windows. In a sudden blast the fresh outside air filled your hermetic room – the afternoon air filled with the smells of the garden, the scent of my roses, the magnolia, the azaleas and the rhododendrons – and I realized that I hadn't felt the summer on my skin until that moment; since your departure I had been living in the shadows. For the first time in a long while, I'd say since the death of Father, I cried. I cried in such a way that I felt relief, lying there on the perfectly made covers of your bed, in that room that there and then felt as distant from me as you had been, my beloved sister.

No, I definitely never knew who you were, Emilie. I knew in the depths of my heart that I had loved and protected you like I had loved and protected no one else in the world, that I had disguised myself as your keeper, your guardian, without ever asking myself why. No reason – I simply did it. There I was all those years, strong and firm enough to protect you as well as myself. But I never knew you, Emilie. Did anyone ever know you?

In these last ten years, with the publication – finally – of your poems, it seems that everyone in Amherst has something to say about you. Everyone has been, to different degrees, confidant, friend, lover or instructor; they all have stories, secrets, or revelatory letters. The Belle of Amherst they call you. The Myth. The timid Miss Dickinson, there, shut away like Bertha in the attic of Thornfield. The Nun of Amherst. The Madwoman of Amherst. The Woman in White who would pass through walls and would go out for walks under the full moon through the midnight town, praying in the empty church when nobody was there to see her, aside from, of course, those fortunate enough to have witnessed such things. The Reclusive Poet. That's the title Colonel Higginson so generously awarded you, and which Mabel has devoted herself to publicizing across the land, so much so that they've even managed to mention it in the editions in which I'm not even acknowledged.

Everyone has a name for you now, but what I found that afternoon in the secretaire where you used to write was, I must confess, utterly unexpected. Curiously it was unexpected even for me, who unlike all those who claim to have *really* known you, have taken the liberty to live by your side fifty-three years, to prepare your funeral according to your instructions, to keep vigil and to bury you. And not only that – God knows not only that.

You, and I've already said this many times, you were the one member of the family who held the post of *thinking*. It's quite true that all of us, Mother, Father, Austin, Sue and even Maggie, we'd all seen you writing for years on those scraps of paper, on the flaps of envelopes, on the backs of shopping lists for the market, everywhere. If you could, I believe you would even have written upon the trees. But as you're well aware, we always were a strange family, everyone living in a separate sector of a labyrinth of few intersections, all in our own world, in our own kingdom behind our own walls. What I mean is that even knowing it, even having seen you, we could never have guessed at the vastness of your legacy.

The afternoon arrived in which you breathed no more, then the long, interminable procession to the cemetery, then the dead time for those of us who were standing. Nobody spoke, nobody remembered what you had lived for – how could they possibly remember that? – seeing that for the past fifteen years you hadn't even shown your face at the door, and seeing that your voice had been no more than the silence of your confinement. Not one of them remembered, Emilie. Not one of them; and I don't blame them, as I myself was amongst their ranks. And yet it was I, two months later, who found your poems, and not just a few verses filed away in any old fashion – no – I found thousands of them, thousands, Emilie, bound like precious objects, catalogued, copied again and again upon papers of differing textures in your hand of twenty years, thirty, forty and fifty. There they all were, divided into fascicles,[3] some lengthy, others unkempt, like good and bad children, all of them orphans.

---

3 "About 1858, according to the best estimates, Emily Dickinson began to assemble her poems into groups, averaging about eighteen to twenty each, which she carefully bound by threading the folded sheets, four or five sheets to each group. There are thirty-nine groups so threaded and four held together with brass fasteners, probably put there by Lavinia. Mabel Todd called them 'fascicles'. The 1955 *Poems* calls them 'packets', a term most recently used to differentiate them from twenty-five other gatherings, not threaded, eight of which appear to have been intended for binding, with seventeen too loosely assembled to judge" [Richard B. Sewall, *The Life of Emily Dickinson Vol II*, Farrar, Straus & Giroux, New York, 1974, p.537]. (Translator's note.)

You dedicated your entire life to creating what you are now. And what you are now, similarly, in my own way, I myself have created.

I'm not deceiving myself, dear sister: I invented you ten years ago.

I'm tired. As well as being old and alone, I'm tired.

I must cope with all the responsibility, with people's vague dying wishes, with the cowardice and misery, as if it were all my own. I must deal with those who are left, and waste the small time I have left keeping the family legacy intact.

I am in a corner: the only thing that protects me is this name that I defend.

Father, Mother, and you are all stones in this cemetery. Grey stones. Deaf stones. And if Maggie follows to the letter the instructions that I have left for my funeral, I will also be one more stone amongst you all. I can almost see my own inscription, upon an identical stone: Lavinia Dickinson, Vinnie Dickinson, or perhaps only: the sister of Emily Dickinson. If I am only remembered as that, I'll die happy, I promise you.

II

It's curious the way God orders events and things in the minds of people. A memory is a far inferior substitute for reality; it's impossible to predict with any certainty what one will remember, and even trying to remember something in particular is rarely effective. We randomly remember things we want to, things we don't want to, some that are useful, and others useless. What is even stranger is the way different people remember the same thing: our childhood, for example, Emilie, Austin, Mother, Father – and myself.

Father would often say: "My son Austin is the eyes, the organs that see. My daughter Emily is the gaze over the world. My daughter Lavinia is the glass in one's spectacles, correcting the fault of one's eyes, focusing one's vision."

Father, for some reason that I'll never know, must have thought that I was very dull.

But maybe I'm being unjust – at times I like to be unjust with the dead – I don't know why, but maybe because of my doubts I've never told anyone about that predisposition of mine to sin. Unjust with Father, who was by no means a bad man – on the contrary – but it was never clear where or how his affection for us would reveal itself, one could only ever guess. We had, how do I say it, the certainty of being loved, but never the feeling of love. Father's love, and also Mother's, was something that passed over one quickly, like the wind passes over the dry branches of the trees in winter, unaffected by them, passing on and leaving as the only proof of its affection a few small piles of snow on the ground.

We knew, in our hearts, of Father's love, but we could never rejoice in it, never allow this wind to sweeten into a breeze to ruffle and caress us. Neither can I think of Father's love as a tree in blossom: nothing could be further from him than the proud, vain fragility of a tree in blossom.

I remember my sister the day Colonel Higginson finally came out to Amherst to visit her, to hear her poetry. She, seated at the piano. He, seated in the rocking chair that I would usually sit in to sew. I had gone to the kitchen to fetch some wine and some gingerbread that Emilie had baked that very morning, interrupting the domestic tasks of everyone in her stubborn determination to have them ready precisely in the afternoon, so that the blasted things wouldn't grow stale. As if some gingerbread could dry up in a couple of hours in a jar! But she was determined, and so I went to the kitchen to put them on a silver tray with a cotton tray-cloth embroidered by Mother, along with some small glasses of redcurrant wine. As I approached the parlour, I overheard Emilie say with a coolness and indifference that I had never before perceived in her voice or mannerism, to a – dare I say it – horrified Higginson:

"I never had a mother. I suppose that a mother is one to whom you hurry when you are troubled, is that not so?"

Well I do not blame her, although at that moment I thought, "how ironic that they should take their drinks off Mother's tray-cloth." And so I returned to the kitchen and removed it. This is how I felt also, but at that moment, before the Colonel, Emilie had already begun to conform to that image of strangeness, of being from another world, which within time others, myself included, would highlight above her other virtues. "She is posing," Austin would say, and I believe he was right.

But Emily was also right in saying that we never had a mother.

III

One night the five of us were eating in the kitchen, a rare occurrence in those days as Austin spent almost all his time in Boston. Father had returned from his office, or wherever he'd been all that afternoon, with a foul temper. That was not a rare occurrence. Father seemed to spend all his days in a bad mood. The important thing is that the five of us were eating together, Father at the head of the table, Mother at the other end – the feet, I would often tell her – Austin at Father's right hand, Emilie at his other, and I, as always, opposite them, alone. In those days I had a healthy appetite, and therefore was never too bothered about being seated beside the bread and dripping. In this way the five of us were solemnly eating. My family always ate solemnly, yet as far as I was concerned solemnity would last only as far as the knife cutting the bread. Mother served the casserole with an exact number of spoonfuls for each of us: twice as much for Father and Austin as for us. Austin and Emilie began to eat and speak at the same time, as they would always do. I, faithful to my own rites, devoted myself to the meagre spoonfuls of casserole fortified with a big hunk of bread spread thickly with far more dripping than a respectable New England young lady should surely tolerate. But back then I was not in the least bothered, just as I was not bothered by so many other things that should have mattered terribly to a girl of fifteen whose chest had only recently begun to push forwards. Aside from that feature, the rest of me was as elemental as anyone of that age would be.

Lord, where was I?... Talking about Father. Father was in a terrible mood, Mother had dished out the casserole, and Father had still not even dipped his spoon in the thick sauce when Emilie and Austin began to eat and talk about I forget which book. Also, in those days, they spoke in code about Sue. Sue Gilbert was part of another story, although very soon she would be part of ours. Anyway, Emilie and Austin would speak in this secret code that at times seemed like a technical discussion of a book of poetry. And I remember Father, with his gaze fixed on his plate, without having eaten even a mouthful. Mother realized but didn't say a word. Mother always realized and never said a word. I never knew why, although at this stage in my life I feel that it was because she was not interested in anything, not even her family, and far less her husband, Edward Dickinson – our Father. I feel that Mother didn't even admire him; she simply followed him, wherever he decided to go, like a sheep following the shepherd, grazing the grass of whichever meadow she is presented with. But that's not important either, not now. Mother said nothing, limiting herself to eating, carefully, her share of delicate spoonfuls. Father then said, in a tone of voice that anticipated a storm:

"Why must I eat out of a chipped plate?"

Emilie and Austin didn't even register Father's complaint, and continued with their whisperings and distracted mouthfuls. I had heard him perfectly, but I looked at Mother, who simply looked down at her plate. There are monsters in her plate, I thought. There is something that looks very like a casserole but is in fact something else, and she knows it and yet eats it all the same. In any respect, Father was also looking down, at his plate; Mother at her plate, and I looked at both of them with a chunk of bread in my hand halfway on its journey from the sauce to my mouth, without daring to dip it for fear of having no time to do something reasonable with it – like eat it. The law of survival, Father would say: every act thought and calculated with the utmost attention. The three of us had heard less, it would appear, than Austin and Emilie. Father then banged his fist so suddenly and loudly on the table that I dropped my chunk of bread out of fright.

"Why must I – why, precisely, must I – eat out of the chipped plate?"

Mother still said nothing. She only managed to direct a glance, both disapproving and fearful, at Emilie, who had been responsible that evening for laying the table for dinner. Austin stopped speaking and looked gravely at all us women in the house – the guilty ones, basically – placing himself on Father's side, in his own ambiguous way, as usual, according to how best it suited him. But Emilie leapt from her seat like a scalded cat, grabbed

Father's plate, casserole and all, and went to the veranda. There, as we could all clearly hear, she smashed the plate on the stone floor. She then came back in, with dark stains of the sauce on her skirt, holding dirty broken bits of china in her hands.

"You'll never again have to eat out of that chipped plate," she said.

Father stared at her as if she were mad.

Mother stared at the stained skirt.

Austin covered his mouth with his hand so as not to laugh.

I stared at them all as if they were on stage and all that was missing was the tragic music.

Emilie stared at Father right in the eyes, holding out the bits of plate like an offering, but in her eyes there was nothing being offered: just pure rebellion.

That was Emilie, my sister, at eighteen: the only one who could stand up to Father in a way that made it impossible for Father to punish her. What could he do? After all, she had obeyed him. Emilie always, always, obeyed in that way: she obeyed while at the same time she rebelled.

I could never do that, especially with Father, and that wasn't because I respected him. When, from the upstairs window we could see him approach the house, his head down and his steps angry, what fun we would have laughing at him. What fun as I mimicked that sullen pace, that tormented expression, that way he had of stepping on the shoots of grass that grew up between the flagstones, annihilating them with his fury.

IV

Ah, watching Father return home! Such a comedy worthy of a London stage. Mother, as soon as she saw him through the window approaching the house, or perhaps simply presuming his arrival owing to the hour, would hastily attempt to prepare all those things that had not been prepared because of errands in town, domestic chores, or books.

"Emily! The table is not laid!"

"Lavinia! How many times have I told you that I don't want to see those cats on the armchairs. And not on the rug either!"

"Austin, dear son. Dirty boots should NOT be in the kitchen, *thank you.*"

"EMILY! That's enough with that book. You can carry on with your reading later. I am your mother and I need some help, right now!"

"Lavinia, for the love of God. Those cats!"

The three of us, or more often us two girls, standing at the window, would attempt to gauge from afar Father's mood, always fluctuating up and down the scale of discontentment. This was always obvious, but we persisted not because we held on to the belief that one fine day Father might come sprightly along the path singing, no, it was because we couldn't conceive of missing the opportunity to mimic him as he arrived – well, me in particular – and to make everyone laugh, even when Mother demanded calm and order or pleaded to the four winds for some help in the house. The kitchen walls could cave in, Emily could fall down the stairs in her haste, and Austin, in his masculine clumsiness, could spill drinks all over the place, but in the midst of all this chaos I would leap to my post to the right of the door to take Father's hat and cane as he came in, and to ensure that once he had finally arrived, a tomb-like silence reigned in the house.

Father, inevitably, would head straight for the thermometer to check the temperature, whilst I, wearing his hat which covered my face and picking my way through the furniture with his cane, would follow him with a dignified air. Emilie, meanwhile, at whichever post she'd been stationed at the instant of Father's arrival, would try to hold back her laughter. In those moments I would make both Austin and Emilie shake with laughter, as I was, and possibly still am as an old woman, the best mimic that I've ever seen in this town. Everyone in Amherst agreed, and they would praise my gift of mimicking people almost as much as they would praise the luminous intellect of my sister. "Vinnie Dickinson has the ability to imitate anyone without embarrassment, even our own Reverend," they would say.

Even in Northampton or in Sunderland my friends would beg me to imitate the untouchables of their towns. But my favourite pastime was to mimic those young ladies of good families yet bad taste to be found in any town, perhaps not so much in the cities, and their matronly mothers, dulled to idiocy from hearing so many sermons in church. When I started to imitate the facial gestures or the body postures of someone, I would be filled with a boldness and self-confidence so strong that I would not even care whom my victims were nor where they came from; neither would I care whether anyone saw me, nor whether I had lost all composure. I was simply transformed into the jester, a position with which I was perfectly content, as I feel that I've always wanted to be just that: the happy jester of the sad king.

Father was a sad king, and I fear that I ended up instead becoming his loyal court treasurer, or his pragmatic war counsellor, his trustworthy vassal and skilled executioner, not just for him but for all the family too.

Spectacles for Austin. Spectacles for Emily – who could be further from being the happy court jester?

V

However, as children we were happy.

Well, as happy as three castaways on a desert island can be happy. Three shipwreck victims who only have each other, a few bananas, one fishing rod, a tree house and an insolent sea that nourishes them and yet separates them from everyone and everything. Yes, we were happy. That oil painting, for example, that still hangs in the entrance hall. The three of us. Austin would have been about seven, Emilie six, and I, as always, three years her junior. Was I really always three years younger than Emilie? It's curious how time changes one's perception of the same differences. Nevertheless, I *was* always the younger. At times I say to myself, whether to remind myself who I am or maybe who I was: I am Lavinia, the youngest of the Dickinsons. Whatever the case, we were happy at one stage, and it's even possible that we were also happy at a later stage – although later death starts to grow alongside you and frightens away happiness. That oil painting, for example: Austin at the back, Emilie and I at the front, the three of us trussed up in suits that would have suffocated us had we had to wear them for more than three minutes. The three of us practically bald, eyes glistening as if with consumption, smiling out of fear, or out of the overwhelming desire to rush outside and play in the park and be left alone. I wonder whether Father had to pay for the execution of such a frightful object as that painting – certainly. Father had even less concept of aesthetics than the artist.

In any respect, it is the sensation of unity that binds me to that horrible painting, or better said that prevents me from throwing it out as I've thrown out so many other things. Our childhood was a type of gift – we were self-sufficient – the three of us would each pretty much play alone, but all the while needing the presence of the other two. By that I mean that the others were not necessarily included in the game, but definitely formed part of the overall scene. Emilie, for example, lived mostly in Lowood, the college for poor orphans where they sent Jane Eyre to remove her from the sight of Mrs Reed, her wicked stepmother. For Emilie, Austin could be, depending on the occasion, Mr Rochester, Mr Brocklehurst, or even that imbecilic cousin John Reed. In general, men were never assigned honourable roles. I was either Bessie, or maybe Miss Temple, while Emilie would vary between being at times Jane Eyre, at times the demented Bertha or even – and this was without doubt her favourite role – Helen Burns. She took to heart with impunity the rebellious nature of Jane, forged out of privations and punishments, because she inclined herself towards extremes, just like Helen inclined towards sacrifice. In both cases, and let's spell it out clearly, the inclination is towards tragedy.

At night, when my sister called me to her room to sleep with her and hug her, it was not Emilie whom I was hugging: it was Helen Burns, abandoned to die sweetly of consumption in her little crib at Lowood.

In this hazy region of daydream Emilie would sink alternately into the pain of rejection, the anguish of hunger, the anxiety of defiance and the horror of lovelessness and death. She lived all of this within her soul, playing out each part, blending it with reality.

Maybe that is why she was able to do so much with so little.

In general, although not always, Emilie's memories were coloured by a special resonance: she felt and experienced everything vividly in her memory, and that which she didn't feel, was simply a space that she filled with whatever she felt should fill it, even if it was not necessarily the truth.

Mother was one of these vacant spaces.

For Austin, on the other hand, memories were of no consequence; indeed the past simply did not interest him. "That which is direct experience," he would always say, "is incorporated into common sense. And that's all it is. That which could not or cannot be naturally assimilated is water that evaporates. And that which is left, that is what *is*. Or what will be." Of the three, Austin has always been the Present. Emily, the Future, the promise. I – I am she who speaks of memories. That's to say, I am the Past. For that reason perhaps I am the one still standing, the one who has buried the rest of her family.

Emilie, as I said, seemed to remember things that had never existed. Or perhaps she transformed them, with that same light that creeps into her writings, that "enchantment", as I call it. There were no greys in her memories, there was none of that insipidness that characterizes mine; the virtues and faults of her memories were not human but those of heroes. They were the memories of Aurora Leigh, of the poor Jane Eyre, the sufferings of Catherine Heathcliff, even the pains of Emily Brontë herself, or of Ophelia, of Hester Prynne...

At times I even imagine that my sister did not *remember* things, but had in fact read them.

In any respect, it has always been the same for us, and that in itself is funny. In that luminous jumble of tragic heroines, rebels and martyrs that weaves itself around her memory, there are elements of reality, vague details – and this is what I find funny – details that I myself cannot remember in the slightest.

In my sister's final years, before becoming entirely bed-ridden, she and I would have a favourite game: we would compare memories of certain events of the past, and reconstruct the event in its entirety. The death of Father, for example, had fragmented irreparably and yet interestingly in our memory, like a puzzle designed by a madman who can and must live without any of the pieces fitting together. Sometimes, however, we would manage to fit some of the pieces together, the most conspicuous ones, the least painful to us, and the result was a beautiful image of Father. The image that appeared was of a sweetness and kindness which, although a little false and unreal, was nevertheless far more vivid and defined than that other hardened image in sepia of the daguerreotype, which was our only visible reference. A little before dying Father had gone to Boston to discuss at the State Legislature the eternal problem of the railroad. The railroad, the college and the Republican Party were his great passions, but he could no longer tolerate the dirty dealings of politics, and his post at the college was in actual practice in the hands of Austin. As a consequence his only remaining passion was the railroad – he had renounced everything else but not this. He was old, tired, but he only allowed this to be seen through tiny gestures, like his rapt absorption in his grand-daughter Mattie, the only member of the Dickinsons who in her early years did not pay him respect.

The afternoon before his departure from Amherst, while I slept, Emilie stayed with Father. She says that they, or more likely merely she, spoke about Shakespeare, and that they, most likely he, spoke about the problems with the railroad and how to expand the routes; and she says that at a particular moment in the conversation Father got up and went to feed the birds. There was nothing in the least unusual about this, as he had a special predisposition towards birds. Indeed birds, unlike anyone else, would often flock around him, ignoring his austere gestures – or is it that birds are unable to recognize the gestures of men? Father seemed so comfortable seated in the kitchen, so at ease that Emilie was quite shocked, and suggested to Austin as soon as he arrived that they go for a short stroll. She says that I, by now risen from my afternoon rest walked with them for a short while before leaving them to perform the various tasks that Mother had asked me to do that afternoon. I remember nothing of any of this. In my view, Father disappeared far earlier, and the most terrible thing about it is that I cannot say with any certainty when it was that I last saw him whole, alive, walking around the house – not as a ghost but as a man. I cannot even recall seeing him feed the birds, as Emilie says. He went away that afternoon and I cannot even remember whether we said goodbye to him or not, despite the fact that Father always said goodbye to everyone, even when the journey was only to be a few meagre miles. It must have happened like that, and in fact both Emilie and Austin remember it to perfection. Mother, as I, only remembered his defenceless body of a few days later.

At that time we could not have much information about his death. Father was stricken with apoplexy after giving his famous speech in favour of keeping the railroad at all costs. He did not die at that very moment, but he died far from us, far from anyone he knew. And now my own part of the memory takes over, crystal clear and precise as only the most abominable memories can be, those memories that one's mind, like a hungry dog, relishes, with the sole purpose of sinking us in sadness. Midway through dinner, Austin arrived. Mother did not rise from her chair: I believe she knew even before Austin spoke. Emilie asked him what had happened, and I, simply upon seeing the terrible

paleness of my brother's face, left the table to prepare
my things. I knew – and moreover I knew that I was the
only one of the family who could accompany Austin. He
said, "Father is extremely ill, we must go to Boston to find
him at once. Vinnie, come with me." At that hour the last
train had already left, and so it was necessary to prepare
the horses. However, we had no time for any of this: while
Austin was giving orders in the stables, the man from the
telegraph office arrived with the message. Father's body
was coming home.

Emilie had chosen to forget about that dinner, about those
thwarted preparations, even about the funeral – although
she had not really forgotten about the funeral as she never
left her bedroom on the day. The house, on the day following
the dinner, was full of people, and it was necessary to have
benches placed in the kitchen and garden, and to use
the kitchen of the Evergreens for the drinks. Our house
simply could not have coped with the amount of people:
everyone from Amherst, absolutely everyone. And the service in the church, and the procession to the cemetery, and
the bewildered faces of Mattie and Ned asking for Grandfather, and Austin with an unhinged expression, crazed,
suffering, pleading me not to leave him alone with all the
preparations, as Mother was not in the right condition to
take charge of anything. I understood him full well. Austin
had been everything for Father, and as the eldest child, he
had reciprocated this affection. I longed to be able to give
him merely one word of support, of strength, but there
were so many people around us and Austin was looking so
uncomfortable. I resisted, but I followed to the letter his instructions for the service. At one moment I slipped out of
the parlour where I had for hours been serving coffee and
cold drinks, and I went up to my room to take a moment

to myself, worn out as I was of seeing endless faces that through weariness I no longer even recognized. Emilie and Austin, in the landing, were weeping and hugging each other. I believe I had never seen them like this, so united, and I believe that never, before or after, had I felt so removed from them, so far away despite all my efforts. At that very moment I felt that I too could weep, for Father as well as for myself, most of all for myself. When Austin saw me he reached out his arm as if to include me in the embrace but I turned on my heels and returned down the stairs. Halfway down I heard Emilie calling me, but I didn't go back upstairs until past midnight.

After Father's death we never again held a Thanksgiving dinner at the house. After Mother's death we never again enjoyed Emily's company at the Thanksgiving dinner held in Austin's house. After my sister's death, I myself have scarcely left the house.

Thanksgiving is for me now a painful date – more than painful – but Father believed in the occasion blindly just like he believed in the stories of our ancestor, the ancient Norman, Walter de Kenson, invader of England, and his succession of lords until the seventeenth century. For Thanksgiving Emilie loved to bake enormous loaves of bread, cookies in the shape of corn, small morsels decorated with fruit, and the famous pumpkin pie. She would always use her own private ingredients, separate from the others and arranged in a part of the kitchen called "the sanctuary" that included part of the old iron Franklin stove. She would never permit anything that wasn't silver to be used for mixing, glass or even crystal glass for measuring, and never, absolutely never, while she mixed or kneaded the dough and the fillings, would she allow herself to deviate even so much as a whisker from the precise measurements of her recipes. Father was the first to ask her to bake the bread and puddings for Thanksgiving. She rarely cooked anything else – that was Mother's role. Emilie would only be found in the kitchen before preparations began, or even after the main meal had been prepared.

How many times have I found poems written on the back of recipes! Or words – simply words.

Phosphorescence
Impalpable
Bud
Ecstasy
Abyss
Amalgam
Rendezvous
Growing
Immortal

And all these words in the same willowy hand as the recipes, with the bars of the T extended across the words like ceilings, with the small silent spaces, empty spaces mysteriously separating one letter from its neighbour, as if by chance, creating more than syllables, forming a series of altered words.

No, since Father's death there were never again any festive Novembers. And yet Emilie continued to prepare her pumpkin pies, each one becoming more elaborate and smaller in size, each one more exquisite and tender, in the shape of birds, butterflies, flowers, woodland gnomes, for Mattie, for Ned and for Gilbert.

Later, much later, Emilie and I would play other games, such as the one of changing identities when I would return from running errands. She would tell me about the goings-on outside, in town, and I would tell her about what had happened in the house, during my absence, behind the closed doors. At those moments she would invent my world, which was *the* world, and I would invent her world, which was simply her.

We were, my sister and I, the most united and yet the strangest sisters that have been. This feeling, I would say, intensified in both directions as time went by, so much so that when she finally stopped breathing I felt that I had finally lost my own breath. So much so that a few months following this, as my pussy cats, who guard my soul, accompanied me, and I was able to enter her room, I finally understood that I had never really known her.

Not I, nor anyone.

2

Maple Syrup (Joseph Lyman)

How dreary 'tis for women to sit still
On winter nights by solitary fires.
— E. Browning, *Aurora Leigh*

I

*T*here was one love in my life, just one true love: Joseph. Joseph Lyman.

I burnt all his letters – I burnt them all in '58, when I finally knew that he had married another woman. The only letters that remain in my possession are those that form part of the correspondence that Emilie and Joseph maintained for a long while. If I keep them it's not for him, but for my sister, because everything related to Emily has become sacred for me.

Joseph was my brother Austin's best friend. He came out to Amherst first during some vacation, and he stayed at our house living out the weeks of recess from Willington College. I was sixteen, he twenty, and our house was still the old house of Pleasant Street. Modest as it was, it seemed to be a luxury mansion to Joseph, and we, the Dickinsons, appeared to him scarcely less than royalty.

Joseph had eight brothers and they were a poor family, made poorer by the lack of a father. He had been brought up on a farm, and he was no stranger to hard manual work. On the contrary, Joseph was easily capable of large working days without breaks, not even for lunch, and sleeping only the few hours necessary. During those days of the recess Austin and he would rise at five, take a quick breakfast and go immediately to feed the horses, then the chickens, and then, after Austin, and not Joseph, had taken a second breakfast of the recently baked morning bread, they would sit down with their study books to prepare for the forthcoming examinations.

Joseph's eagerness and enthusiasm for books, for knowledge in general, had drawn him immediately to Emily. At that time, though, Emily was just one more of the many girls of Amherst, only far less glamorous and far more intelligent than the others. She didn't dress in white, and in general her clothing seemed to be of no importance to her and she never devoted any time to doing up her hair. This was certainly due to Mother's feeling that dresses and coats should be sewn only when ripped, and washed only when dirty; whether the clothing was in good or bad taste, whether this or that sunhat was currently in fashion, none of this mattered in the least to Mother. Emily had inherited from Mother this same doleful appearance, this same instinctive indifference, even disdain, for clothes, and yet Emily – not because she didn't know how to appreciate beauty, on the contrary – was always the first to recognize the quality of muslin in the outfit of other girls, or the excellence of a shawl embroidered with silk thread, or the elegance of a girl's curls held up with velvet ribbons and small cotton flowers. Therefore Emily's practices were a mixture of both upbringing and indifference, and perhaps that is why Joseph felt an immediate spiritual connection with her, but nothing more.

From '46 onwards, from his first visit to Amherst until the spring of '51, Joseph's visits to the house were frequent. I would go to the door to greet him, and then again to bid him farewell when he left with Austin. At that time I had nothing more than friendly words, attentive remarks, simple coquetries that so appealed to him. We would go out with the pony and trap for trips around the area, we would have picnics in the woodland, ride out on the horses, and we would read, above all we would read, sitting in the garden in the warm afternoon sun surrounded by the flowers of May and June, with the watchful eye of Mother and Father always upon our backs; with Emily interrupting us to argue with Joseph the merits of some new novel, while the poor fellow struggled through my classes of Virgil; with certain sketches in German that I could never fathom beyond a ragged *guten morgen*; with tender tales of his poor childhood, and vague intuitions about the future.

We grew to know each other very well, and although my primordial speech was never intellectual, this delighted Joseph more than anything else. He used to say to me, "Vinnie, everything is abstraction, everything: air, water, scent, the mathematical formulae that I read, this very book, its paper, everything is merely words and words are abstractions. Everything save the way that you have of placing your hand in mine. Everything save that way you have of letting your hair tumble freely over your back, and the way you have of resting your head upon my shoulder."

It was natural that we should love each other, as natural as it was childlike and pure. There was no meanness. What we shared was hidden from Father and Mother, but Emily always kept herself abreast, as did Austin, of course. We would tarry upon our treks, a few yards behind the others, or we would push on in front, or we would seek some excuse to plunge into some hidden corner of the woodland that we both knew of, where we could be alone to enjoy our conversations.

A number of years passed in this way.

As an adolescent, during that mysterious age of joy and pain and enormous irresponsibility, one never notices the passing of time. One only begins to notice time, as I notice it now, upon growing old. Every hour, every minute I feel time slipping away, but back then I never did, back then time was of no consequence, we had thousands of hours, days and years before us.

Father and Mother would often call us *the young folks*. "And what have the young folks been up to today?" Father would ask from the porch as he awoke from his immutable and sacrosanct afternoon nap. We, in reciprocation, would call them *the old folks*. "The old folks are off to Boston this morning!" proclaimed Austin with enthusiasm. "The Mansion is ours!" And the Mansion was indeed ours, our own Gondal, our own Angria. There were impromptu parties to which the young of various houses of the surrounding area would be invited, friends who laughed at Emilie's extraordinary conversations and at my imitations of illustrious members of the community. Yes, those years were certainly the best, the happiest in an absolute sense, the most happy that I can remember. But school would soon be completed and the need to "make plans for the future", from that bundle of indescribable promise that was the future of such a young country, lay in wait for us, just as did adulthood, the old age of others, illness, the death of loved ones – reality.

The spring of '51 marks the end, or perhaps the beginning, of another stage: that of waiting. Joseph had graduated from Yale, and in March he came to visit us for the last time: he had decided to seek his luck and his fortune in the South. During those days, trying our best to ignore a fact that we both knew to be irreversible, we planned – as everyone wanted us to – absolutely everything, from a romantic elopement and a secret marriage, to swearing and committing ourselves to love and patience. Two years – that is what Joseph said. Two years was too long, but, although I was not aware at the time, two years would be nothing compared to the fourteen years that would pass before I saw his tousled red hair again. And that time would be the last time. No, there was no way I could have known, and I naively placed my trust in life, in tolerance, in patience, and above all in love. Love, I would repeat to myself every night, was a divine sentiment, a sacred and blessed gift from God, magnificent and eternal.

I was still a child, a child of long black hair like the wings of a crow, with innocent eyes that would change with the sky, sometimes grey, sometimes green, sometimes the colour of honey; and my body was without blemish, white, fresh and soft. I had no qualms about approaching with my red ottoman to sit beside Joseph, as he sat absorbed in his reading, letting my hair down to lie about his lap, leaning my back against his legs or to hug him fiercely.

Nothing serious or sad had yet occurred to us, and that is why I understand that it is at times unjust to talk about an unhappy childhood or about a life worn down by lovelessness. It was not like that, and in this Emily was perfectly correct: home was, and has always been, something sacred for the Dickinsons. Nothing untoward could ever happen to us there, nothing that could make us lose faith in the goodness and nobility of humankind, nor lose faith in the future. Nothing could expose us to the storm outside, it was our private and fantastic kingdom, and we inhabited it naturally, like fairies do in tales, or those rebellious and passionate beings in novels.

But soon we learnt that the walls were not impregnable. We all learnt: Austin in his own way, Emily in hers, and I for my part, learnt thanks to Joseph.

That spring was the last that we were to spend together. I remember, more than the plans and reckless and wild

ideals, an afternoon excursion from Amherst to Montague,
to the most remote woodlands near Mount Sugarloaf, for
the maple syrup harvest, known as the sugaring-off party.
The party consisted of a number of young people, and some
adults who were coming along as chaperones, riding in a
cart adorned with flowers – a happy and almost summery
group. Joseph, in his desire for secrecy and concealment,
tarried alongside Emilie, talking about Heaven knows
which classic German writers. I was happy for him to do
this, knowing that at a certain moment of general confu-
sion, probably during the cooking of the syrup, he and I
would find the time to run off alone amongst the oldest
maples. This event was something of an initiation rite for
the young – Joseph and I would take it one step further.

The beginning of spring, but especially the month of
March, is the maple syrup season, when the winter snows
begin to melt, the final cold spells are less cold, and the days
little by little are longer than during the winter. Nowadays,
nearly at the turn of the century, the process is not carried
out entirely outdoors, but back then, those excursions into
the woods were, principally, in order to cook the syrup of
the first day of the harvest, officially marking the beginning
of the sugar season.

The history of the maples is a beautiful one. Throughout
the summer, and thanks to the sun that for so many hours
bronzes the tree canopy, sugars begin to accumulate in
the leaves, which later are converted into sap, amassing
like treasure in the trunks of the trees. This is the sweet
soul of the maple. Towards the end of summer and during
autumn, the maple sheds these very leaves that have acted
as sponges, soaking up the sunlight. These leaves – some
reddish, others yellowish – fall with the first frosts. Then,
throughout the winter the tree simply survives, and its
sweet soul of sap, protected behind layer after layer of

living tissue, dead pulp and bark, remains intact, becoming sweeter and sweeter while the snow builds up on the dry, dead-looking branches and against the sleeping trunks; and the farmers keep the surrounding area clear so that should a tree fall it should not damage one of the young maples.

Then spring arrives, and thanks to the sweet sap hidden away on the inside, the maples return to life; the new shoots appear timidly to greet the sun that slowly grows more and more yellow, and this is when the work of the sugar-maker really begins: the maple harvest. Sometimes, if spring comes early or if winter has not been too severe, the operation begins in the middle of February, but normally the maple harvest is during March, although there is no one simple and precise sign: the time is usually called the "sugar season". Some believe that the sugar season is announced during the day by the crows, unable to wait in silence for the arrival of warmth.

The sugar men know exactly where, amidst the dense woodlands, the edible syrup is to be found: it takes forty years for a tree to grow from planting to sugar production. The men head off to these places with the sledges, as snow is still thick in the drifts, armed with wooden pails girdled to perfection with metal rings. The night before the first harvest they hang these pails outside the cabins full of hot water, then cold water, so that the wooden slats swell into each other, helping to seal them. And they go, with their sledges, their pails and their tools, to bore into the maples a hole no more than three inches wide, three feet up, like a small wound through which the soul of the tree willingly bleeds. The healthiest and largest of the maples will tolerate up to three of these holes, and the sugar-men try never to wound the tree twice in the same place, always allowing the wounds of the previous year to scar over completely. The pails hang from the spouts and they are left to collect the clear sap that drips down, slowly at first, then as time goes by, much quicker, until there is none left. When the pails are full, their collective contents are poured into enormous boilers, and either fires are lit in special spots in the forest, or the pails are carried to the cabins, where a more industrialized system helps to evaporate the water from the sap. In the forest, when the harvest is small, the dense liquid is poured into metal receptacles that are placed like gigantic kettles above the fire, boiling the syrup. And when it is at the right point, it can be thrown onto the snow, where the syrup acquires its wax-like consistency. If two drops melt as they fall, it means that the syrup is ready to be jarred.

And in this way, each spring, pails are hung from their small taps, and the maples, day after day, continue with their slow and sweet bleeding.

It was during this excursion that I learnt that Joseph had made plans to go to the South, to New Orleans, the city of Spanish gypsies with dark almond-shaped eyes; the city of slaves, the city where the *grandes dames* of society, faces hidden behind porcelain and glitter masks, take part in elaborate rituals of black magic; the city of easy money, turmoil and unrest: the perfect city for Joseph.

He went during that spring.

The Civil War was at this stage nothing more than angry conversations about certain stubborn and powerful southern states, and the urgent need for a workforce in the industries that were being born in the North.

Soon after setting himself up there, Joseph met Laura Baker, of Tennessee, a lady of quality who, according to him, and perhaps according to anyone of any astuteness, possessed all the qualities that I neither had nor ever shall have.

I waited for him, and while I waited I received nothing more from him than a few ambiguous letters in which he assured me that he would return to marry me.

I waited for him, foolishly, whilst everything was clearly pointing to the fact that it was futile; until Emily, who for such things was always reserved, said to me: "Vinnie, that's enough: Joseph is engaged to be married," and she gave me one of his letters addressed to her, in which Joseph mentioned as if in passing – "tell Vinnie too" – that Laura Baker had agreed to marry him.

Laura Baker was still alive when Emily died, and that was the last I knew of her, for she sent me her condolences in a precise and formal card. You see the hypocrite was also good, as good as even little Lucy Thurston, who being so good went directly to heaven when she died.[4]

II

Now our young love seems no more than a dream, something gentle and balsamic, like feeling the summer breeze on the hilltops of Pelham. Why, Joseph, did we have to grow up? How much I would love for us to be young again, that this battle of life had never begun!

Why did you tell me in a couple of lines of trivial conversation that you had got engaged to someone else? Why did you not even send that letter to me, but to Emily? What would happen if we could suddenly find ourselves together,

---

4   Lucy Thurston was the protagonist of an old lullaby, which literally went: "Lucy was so good that when she died she went straight to heaven". For the strict puritans, accustomed to rousing sermons about purgatory and eternal punishment, to go straight to heaven constituted the highest spiritual achievement. (Author's note.)

face to face once again, after so many years and so many useless words?

Tell me, Joseph, what do you think would happen?

> What you love,
> Is not a woman, Romney, but a cause:
> You want a helpmate, not a mistress, sir,
> A wife to help your ends in her no end!

If I'd had the courage to tell Austin about what had happened that afternoon on the sugaring-off excursion to Montague, he never, never, would have allowed you to go, Joseph. Not over his dead body, I knew him well. Not for me – don't fear, I'm not so credulous – but he would have done it nevertheless, and I would have benefited from it. I didn't tell him, and for that reason I've repented as often as I've been glad. At this stage in my life I feel that it was best to lose you. If my body, which was all that I had in my youth, was not enough to hold you, it is unlikely that my conviction would have done so, nor the strength of my affection, nor my scarce virtues. My body was what I had to offer, and I gave it to you, and in this the two of us have lost: I, because since then mine has been a barren life, and you, because you decided to follow your ambition even after knowing what my heart would have unconditionally given you.

I know that you have spoken crazily about me all these years: Emily has told me so, for she has known what it is like to receive the letters that you, and later your wife, would send. I know that to Laura Baker I must appear odious, superficial and vain, a woman of few virtues and even fewer faults to boast of, an image of the past that you have returned to again and again with either venom or enthusiasm according to which suited you best.

No, I would never have wanted to be in Laura Baker's skin. What's more, at times I feel sorry for her, and even feel stronger than her – I, the clandestine lover with empty hands – a sad power that I wasn't even able to wield as it was based upon weakness and pride or the whims of a lover – but power all the same. I imagine that Laura Baker has suffered more than one migraine, more than one sweat of fear thanks to an uttered memory of Joseph, and I imagine that she has at times felt herself superior to me for the selfsame reason.

I will admit, I am not proud of any of this, but thanks to Joseph's selfishness this has not been my responsibility.

Some time following the letter that Emilie received, I myself sent him another letter in which I gave him all my love and support, only asking that I may see him, that we may see each other, once, just once, before he consummated the marriage with Laura Baker. As a reply, he sent me these lines that I still keep, not on paper, but in my memory:

> Better to have loved and lost
> than never to have loved at all.

In memoriam for our love, of course. That very afternoon anger made me accept the offer of a pretender from Northampton, earning me one of Father's rages, disapproving looks from Mother and Austin when they found out, and considerable patience to try to untie this promise with someone who was not worth a fig to me. Right at this moment I cannot even recall his name.

III

Before setting off, Joseph told me that in order for us to marry we would have to earn a thousand dollars annually. I replied that it wasn't necessary – at least for me – to live like a queen if only I was living by his side. He said that it wasn't a question of living like a queen, but of *being* a queen. Joseph's ambition knew no bounds. Here, for example, in this letter that he wrote to my sister, he says, likewise almost in passing (everything with Joseph, I only came to realize too late, was in passing): "Vinnie is like Ophelia: she has lost her Lord Hamlet through not understanding him, through not rising to his level."

Can anyone possibly believe such smugness? I, of course, never said anything when he compared himself with Julius Caesar, with Napoleon, with kings and gods of all calibre – but Hamlet! He, Hamlet, and I, Ophelia... oh for Heaven's sake!... even Emily could have responded to such audacity. No, his ambition was simply brash and shameless, no more no less. What is certain is that in his eyes, in matters of intellect, I was no more than a fussy young girl, worried about frocks and bonnets and tea parties, while he, Caesar, was far, far above such banalities.

As soon as I heard about his death I wrote a brief letter of condolence to Laura Baker, and I asked her for Emily's and my letters, if, that is, Joseph still had them in his possession. Amongst those aged papers I found some letters that Emily and I had sent in the year 1855, the very year that we moved to this house.

I was twenty-two and I still believed that Joseph would return for me.

Amherst, 13th October 1855

My dear Joseph,

After so long waiting, & after so very much work, yesterday we finally moved into our new house. As you know, the house belonged to Grandfather Samuel, which, as for us, is probably how you would remember it – Old Dickinson's Mansion. But now it is honestly almost a new house, Joseph. Father has been working hard over the last few months overseeing the changes & renovations with the firm of Boston architects, Howe, Manning & Almy, a suitably traditional firm, good people, & as far as the works testify, understanding; (I also believe that Father has only been able to pay them because they were his clients in a lawsuit some time ago.) In truth, we have all been working very hard in this since we returned from Washington. Even Emily launched her own attack on the rugs & carpets, which had to be moved to the new house only after first repeating the odious annual ceremony of airing & beating them in the sun. Are these details too domestic, perhaps?

The house looks like Phoenix Hall – there are scarcely any brick houses in Amherst. Have you noticed that?

The external masonry, & the columns at the front entrance are white, the same as the balustrade & banisters of the stairway. The ground floor, as you come in, opens up with a hall with the closed double parlour to the left, the library to the right, which I can already assure you will become the favourite place of you-know-who. The parlour also extends to the back of the house, with windows giving on to such a beautiful garden, Joseph, which I do hope you'll be able to see soon – or perhaps not so soon – let me work a little upon those poor neglected flowers... Anyway, as I was saying, to the right of the hall, between the reception rooms, runs a narrow corridor that leads to the dining room, which is at the end of the west wing, to the incredibly spacious pantry in which you could store enough provisions for a number of winters or for an entire regiment – &, lastly, to the kitchen, wash room & ultimately to the scullery. These three rooms also give on to the garden, & there is running outside the windows a small veranda, which I will also bedeck with flowers – you'll see. There is a stairway that leads up from the hall to the first floor, & there is also a back stairway which leads up from the kitchen & pantry. The bedrooms are upstairs; mine & Emily's are of the same dimensions & both look out over the front, & at the end of the corridor that separates them there is a perfect little balcony. The bedroom that will now not be Austin's is behind Emilie's, & over the west wing, that's to say, over the dining room, is Mother & Father's room. There is still an attic, but Father doesn't believe that it will be finished before next summer, even with luck. As such the attic is at present no more than a cold empty space, with a cupola that Emily wasted no time in christening "the bewitched chapel". It has eight windows, two in each wall, & from there, I assure you, you can see absolutely all of Amherst, the hills of Pelham, even as far as Belchertown & the other side of the river. Do you not miss the banks of the Connecticut, Joseph? Remember how you & Austin would go fishing for those tadpoles, & at times even toads that you would bring back to the house, proud of having caught something?

I suppose that the life of the South must also have rivers – the Mississippi is not to be deplored – it's just that, as they say, its waters are too green, & that the insects that breed there are more bothersome than the floods & rains. I wonder if that is true. I even wonder whether you've been to the river to fish, like you did here. These New England rivers are very predictable, are they not? They rise in the spring, they are eaten up by ice & snow in winter, & that is basically the biography of the river, season after season. Oh, but why have I forgotten about the house? It is, Joseph, a true mansion; the wallpaper is perhaps a little too pale & classical. You'll have seen that nowadays blues & burgundies are preferred to pale colours, but Austin was unable to convince Father to change his mind about the walls. The architects were also unable, so it would appear – & so there we are, surrounded by a fairly lunatic brightness. We brought over all the furniture from the house at Pleasant Street – all of it – & so far we've not bought anything new, save some carpets bought from Merchant's Row to fit the dimensions of the dining room. Austin has gone into partnership with Father, did he tell you that? If not he will soon. Father is determined to build him a "special" house, in a plot he acquired a short distance from here, almost sharing the same garden. All that would separate the houses would be a sparse woodland & a flagged path that is already built. Emily burns with joy to know that Sue & Austin are to marry, & that they will certainly accept the offer to live here. Austin certainly, but I am not so sure about Sue – she is so independent, so much one to forge her own existence – well, you know her. But my sister lies awake knowing or hoping that Sue will be nearby. They say that they will marry next year, in the summer, in Geneva, New York. Father is not so keen on this idea, & I don't think Austin is either. But Sue is stubborn, & so it's most likely that she'll have her way.

Oh, but I am boring you. It's months since I last wrote so much, & my fingers now ache from clutching the pencil, which I've now sharpened about four times – I've worn away so much of it for you, on this paper. Are you not proud of your Vinnie in her new role?

Dear, dear, darling Joseph, how I wish you were here, & that you could see these wonders with your own eyes. As Emily says, home is a sacred place, & this home doubtlessly is that. I can't wait for you to return here, & for us to resume our walks, our reading in the sun, for you to resume patiently teaching me that inaccessible language.

& I've not written anything, I know, about our friends. I am such a miser, but I want you to know that they all remember you with great affection. I need not tell you about Emily because from here I can see her writing to you herself. We will put our respective letters in the same envelope that I wish could fly like a swift to New Orleans, that city of ghosts in which you live, that city of rivers green like snakes, of tropical heat & decay. Am I right? It's only because I read about it recently. Joseph, promise me that you will write & that you will come back here as soon as you've saved the "capital" you feel we need. Promise me that, Joseph, & I will then go with you to wherever you wish – to Madeira or to the Isle of Juan Fernandez – I don't care.

With my everlasting love,

Your Vinnie

I find some pretty striking things in this letter. It seems so remote and strange, for example, to imagine Austin and Sue so happy planning their future lives. And Joseph. And my exuberance about the house, an emotion that I still feel today when I go up to the bewitched chapel with Maggie, a secret spot that was never refurbished. And it remains Emily's secret place – and she, who in a manner that I could not explain even if I wanted to, remains up there, frozen in time, floating between those eight sacred windows, lit up at the same time by the landscapes beyond the windows.

The afternoon in which we were both writing our respective letters to Joseph on the recently-moved table, Emily was composing her own laconic résumé about various topics that have no relevance now.

By the way, Joe, we've moved house. It's been many days of intensely hard and tiring work, literally lifting the carpets from the floor and cleaning them until our backs would

break. Perhaps I have in reality always preferred pestilence.
With regard to the house, I imagine that Vinnie will have
filled you in with all the details.

IV

Not three months had gone by since Lincoln took power,
when the Southern States declared themselves Confeder-
ates and resolved not to join with the rest of America. There
were seven states in all, including Mississippi, Carolina
and Georgia, and others that would join them later. Lincoln
called for volunteers to participate in the Anaconda Plan in
the Gulf of Mexico, and in '62 the Civil War had officially
begun.

The North was emptied of its menfolk. In Amherst the
young men were enlisting voluntarily, and those who
couldn't go to fight for the freedom of the slaves paid the
federal government a fee to maintain the regiments or
to rebuild destroyed cities. Joseph, having lived for many
years in the South, had begun to send suspiciously neutral
letters with regard to slavery, until finally, in a more public
dispute, he ended up admitting that the system of slavery
worked in an acceptable way for the southern economy.
Father got wind of these opinions, as he got wind of most
things that happened in town, and I knew that thereafter I
could not count on Father's blessing – assuming, that is, that
I still could count on the word of Joseph to return for me.

  During that time, in which correspondence would fluc-
tuate in accordance with the victories and defeats of the
armies, Joseph wandered through various states engaged
in various jobs, as a reporter when his luck was good, as
a reconstruction builder most of the time. He would write

about what he witnessed with an unexpected bitterness, at times brutally or even spitefully. All his dreams and fantasies about wealth and prosperity were slipping away, just like the once-powerful opulence of the plantations, and as the battles raged leaving nothing but ashes, Joseph saw his own ruins amidst the rubble.

When the war ended, Joseph was left with empty hands.

The South, the land in which he had flourished, was devastated. All his ambivalent opinions about slavery and the abolitionists, all that he had displayed in his letters and newspaper articles, in his conversations and embittered responses to those who were seriously interested in the theme – all this was not going to help him upon his return to the North. When he returned he was unable to find work, and eventually went to live with his mother in Easthampton, slightly under twenty miles from Amherst.

Throughout the whole of '64 he did what he could, which was not much, while his wife and children (there were about five children at that stage) moved in with her family in Somerville. We suspected then that the war had created some hidden rift between him and Austin, because he never came to see us despite declaring his desire to visit "his dear old friends of Amherst" in more than one letter, especially those addressed to Emily. We knew very little about him, no more than what he would tell us, and we had long ago lost the hope of receiving him at home ever again. Father and Mother were still living at that stage, and perhaps it was not so much out of fear of Austin, but of Father, that Joseph never plucked up the courage to visit, seeing that the topic of slavery had upset Father in an unexpectedly forcible way.

By the new year, as I said, we had already lost all hope. But it turned out that Joseph did land himself a job as an editor for the New York newspaper *The Tribune*, thanks to a contact of a certain Mr Cramwell or Cromwell, who right at that moment, was passing through Amherst on his direct way to New York. In February of '65 Joseph packed his bags and left Easthampton for the last time, visiting Amherst, with the obvious excuse of sharing the journey with Mr Cramwell. There was no time for spectacular preparations, nor was there more forewarning than a few hours, but before we knew it, Joseph's carriage, laden with all his luggage, was outside our house. I believe that it was a blessing that Father and Mother were in Northampton until later that afternoon, one of those work commitments that so bored poor Mother but that she was unable to turn down. That's not important now. They were not at home, and Austin had left for Boston with Sue and the child.

Emily and I were alone when Joseph came to the door. A gentle snow had sadly begun to fall. When I opened the door, Joseph was standing there on the threshold, looking at me without saying a word. Neither could I speak, and for a few moments I tried to reconstruct in my mind the image of that thin young man, his clear blue eyes, unkempt clothing, and impulsive manners, who had said farewell to me in that very place fourteen years earlier. There was now nothing left of that youth, now there was a man standing before me. Thin as before, perhaps the result of excessive work, which had curved his back prematurely, giving him the appearance of an old man. He suddenly shifted on his feet, timidly entered the hall and took off his cape. He was wearing spectacles, and he wore a suit of the style not then in vogue, unless that was merely the clothing they all wore in the South – I don't know. There was nothing unkempt about him, on the contrary, Joseph was dressed like a courtier. Then the spell of memory broke, and politely I invited him into the parlour. He had never been in the new house, and yet he gazed at everything with nostalgia, as if he were reaching back into memories of having been there, or as if he were lamenting not being once again at the old house of Pleasant Street.

I remember that he said:

"It's far more impressive than your description in the letter."

"Well I never was very good at describing things I like," I replied.

He then asked after my sister, and I replied that I would go to the kitchen to prepare tea and some gingerbread that Emily had baked specially for the occasion.

"And she?" insisted Joseph. "Is she not at home?"

I limited myself to slipping away to the kitchen. I knew perfectly well that my sister was on the backstairs, the stairway that connected the kitchen with the first floor. At the base of the stairs on the ground floor there was a little hall which led to the kitchen, to the passage and to the parlour. Perhaps from the parlour it would be difficult to detect her, but I knew perfectly well that Emily was there, on the stairs, making certain that she could hear everything without being seen.

I tried to keep my hands from trembling, as at that moment I was not at all concerned about Emily's strange behaviour but about how my own meeting with Joseph would unravel. In many respects the fact that Emily was not present was a burden to me, as my repertoire of acts of etiquette was very limited, and I was not particularly skilled at performing them for very long. When I returned, Joseph was staring out of the window at what could be seen of the Evergreens, Austin and Sue's house.

"And Austin?" he asked.

"In Boston, on business," I replied. "With maple syrup, as always?"

I believe that I did it on purpose, although not with malice. My heart was aching too strongly for me to be capable of irony or malice. He realized this, for he replied with his head lowered:

"Thanks, but now I cannot take anything sugary."

I sat at the table, facing him – two adults with nothing to say to each other. In order to break the silence Joseph began to speak of the war, and he told me that he was writing a book about what he had seen and lived through. I asked him how his newly born daughter was, and he raised a surprised eyebrow, as if he couldn't imagine that I would know anything about his life with Laura Baker. It was a false note of surprise, of course. He said that she was fine, and that soon he would be bringing his family down to New York to join him, as soon as he was settled there. He said that he had a great future ahead of him as a journalist, that his articles about the war had been immediately published and that he was trying to dedicate himself exclusively to opinion editorials. I asked him if he saw me very changed, and again, like the former question, he raised that eyebrow, another gesture of false ignorance. But he replied that yes, that now I was a woman whereas before I had only been a child. I chose not to enquire any further, but at that moment Emily, or rather Emily's white skirt, appeared on the bottom stairs. I rose and went up to her: she handed me a tray with a glass of wine and a folded note.

"For Joe," she said simply, and turned back up the stairs.

From the parlour Joseph had seen everything, I am certain, but when I returned to the table he said nothing about the occurrence.

"Emily sends you this, with all her love and affection," I said mechanically and handed him the small tray.

He ignored the wine but at once unfolded the paper. Something brief – a poem no doubt.

"Is she all right?" he asked.

"As always," I replied. "The same Emilie as always, Joseph. We are all more or less the same as always, just grown a little."

"Yes," he said. "I'm sorry."

I didn't ask him what it was that he was sorry about. I myself was already so sorry about so many things that were not worth even mentioning that I simply remained silent.

After some minutes Joseph declared that the snow had turned to sleet, and that if it should freeze then the journey would be dangerous. He rose, and he went alone to retrieve his cape from the hall. He then asked me to thank Emily for the gingerbread (which he hadn't tried) and for the note. He took my two hands in his, kissed them, and promised to write to the both of us.

When I closed the door I could no longer contain my tears – nothing – absolutely nothing had happened.

Well that's what I believe now that so much time has passed since that occasion. And yet I do believe that something important did happen then: that was the first time, or at least the first that I remember with total clarity, that my sister received a close friend from the stairway, without actually being physically present during the conversation, without allowing anything beyond the hem of her white skirt to be seen. That obsession with wearing white began much later, but on that occasion, by chance, or perhaps because her tendency for oddity had already begun to manifest itself, Emily dressed in white. I didn't ask her why; I myself was going through great pains to hold back my anger and anguish, not to break down and cry like a little girl, nor to hurl myself into Joseph's arms as Aurora would have thrown herself into the arms of Romney. I was so engrossed in holding on to myself that, although I had seen her and noticed the fact quite clearly, I asked her nothing – I let it pass.

That was a mistake, certainly. Later, compelled by her and by routine, we would all grow accustomed to those disproportionate attitudes of Emily, we would learn to incorporate them into the habit of the house like a natural force, and when we finally realized, it was too late to ask for explanations, as that would have made *us*, and not her, appear insane.

On that occasion I delayed asking her why she had deprived Joseph of her presence but not of her generosity. Who knows whether she would have ever answered me. All I know is that it was the first time that my sister hid herself from a visitor, that this visitor in question was Joseph – my Joseph – and that from that moment on that custom of hers would become one of the most remarkable features of the eccentric Miss Dickinson – my sister Emily.

It would be better for me to say that I never saw Joseph again after that spring excursion – that farewell to that youth of ours, so full of promises. Even the meeting in Amherst could very well have occurred only in my memory: Emilie, for example, never wrote a word about the occasion – that I or anyone could testify – and we never again spoke about him, not even in passing.

The only thing that is absolutely certain is that he wanted to triumph, and *that* is why he left.

He died of smallpox in his house on Long Island.

3

A Sensitive Plant (Emilie)

...This same world
Uncomprehended by you must remain
Uninfluenced by you. Women as you are,
Mere women, personal and passionate,
You give us doting mothers, and chaste wives.
Sublime Madonnas, and enduring saints!
We get no Christ from you – and verily
We shall not get a poet, in my mind.
— E. Browning, *Aurora Leigh*

I

She was seated at the dining-room table, holding a violet pencil, with an indefinable expression, staring at me. I had just entered from the kitchen bearing a basket containing the tablecloth and the plates in order to lay the table for lunch.

"Tiny crystals of unexpected sorrow," she absently muttered, all the while gazing at me.

"Tears!" said I.

Emilie said nothing.

"Dewdrops!" I tried again.

Silence.

"Sweat?" I offered now without hope.

"Tiny crystals," said Emily with a bored tone of voice. "Nothing more than tiny crystals, tiny tiny crystals."

Everything was like that with Emilie. On those days when complex issues seemed to her pointless, she would opt for this mask of simplicity, or simple-mindedness, in such a way that nearly everything would appear clumsy, foolish and trivial. And yet, this triviality was precisely the first and almost only thing she would reject, that she would not even consider for somebody's sake in particular – and if that somebody perhaps lacked the sensitivity to read between the lines, that person was not worthy of joining her circle of souls.

Sometimes I feel that Emilie was ostensibly selfish, as she would always take advantage of the simplicity of others, making herself stand out, giving herself a separate identity – an identity like some sort of trophy, only earned through fighting, all too easily, with the average person. Also, I must confess, I have many times felt myself far from this majestic circle where everyone aside from Emilie would play mindless games that appeared no more than riddles, more appropriate to the confused or disconcerted than to the lucid.

Emilie always denied this, especially during her final years, with the stubbornness of a mule – but I know that she always felt this urgent need to transcend, to be accepted as a poet, to be admired, to be famous. But in a veiled and enigmatic way she wanted more to be "distinguished". Famous or distinguished – it's all the same. And what's wrong with that?

I myself shared this sense of ambition, but not to be a poet: I wanted to be an artist, an actor on the stage, to be like Sarah Bernhardt, to accompany the great Tommaso Salvini or to sing like Jenny Lind, to receive a standing ovation, as she did, following her performance *a cappella* from the tower of the Boston Hotel to all those members of the public who had been unable to enter the theatre... Ah, how I would have loved to have played Lady Macbeth, Violetta Valeri, Leonora or Desdemona – even Carmen herself! How I love the opera, concerts – and I never even knew how to sing. I could also barely play the piano, beyond those simple pieces that one devotes such time to learning in one's youth in order to impress others, only later to forget.

But I honestly felt like someone else when I gazed at myself in the mirror, seeing my reflection spin lies, inventing for my solace a stage in New York, Boston or Washington, a stage with its heavy dark purple velvet curtains, the theatre like a castle, or a fantasy park, with its boxes hidden in the shadows behind folds of brocade, elegant ladies concealed behind stern opera glasses, gentlemen with lascivious looks, and the majestic dome decorated with delicate frescos like a pale sky rising above the orchestra and the audience, and then the sublime silence, the first chord of the violins...

And then Father or Mother would call me to carry out some mundane task, and there would be Austin with his jokes and Emily with her look of gracious surprise or false solemnity. I saw myself alongside Jenny Lind, at times even combing my hair back like hers into a fairly tight bun – my hair being black and straight like hers – and I would lower my shoulders, pull down the neckline of my dress as far as the incline of my chest, put around my neck a brooch on a velvet ribbon – and there I was – *The Swedish Nightingale!* – until, that is, surrendering to an irrepressible urge, I would force out the first tone of a laboured soprano, and the whole illusion would collapse to be replaced with the humble reality of our house.

Despite that, I always thanked the imaginary audience with a deep theatrical bow, while my *partenaire*, the great Tommaso Salvini, would hold my hand, and together, amidst applause and flowers raining upon the fantasy stage, we would leave this small, sumptuous and happy world where nothing and nobody were as they seemed.

In the summer of '51, following Joseph's departure – impossible not to know the date exactly: 3rd July, impossibly hot and humid New England summer – Jenny Lind sang in Northampton, at the Edwards Church, as part of a tour that had begun in New York the previous year. From the moment she arrived in America her concerts caused an uproar on all sides, to the extent that, although the tour had not been scheduled to take in more than the big cities, they were compelled to extend it to twice the original bookings owing to stampedes provoked by Jenny's mere presence.

That afternoon the "family committee" set off from Amherst. By that I mean everyone save Austin, who was in Boston teaching and who anyway had already attended her famous performance at the tower of the hotel. Emily and I were dressed as if for a wedding, so much so that we suffered reprimands from Father on the journey towards the bridge, which, owing to what then followed, we were able simply to ignore.

The first thing to mention is the horses. Even as we were leaving town we could see, and feel, that the horses were of a nervous and spoilt type, but Father chose to overlook this, and signalled to the driver that everything was fine, that the family were all settled in the carriage and that he should proceed. As we approached the Connecticut river, near the bridge, the storm began – the typical treacherous summer storm that blackened the skies in a couple of minutes, stirring the inoffensive breeze into a howling wind, and bringing on thunder and lightning to proclaim the rain. By the time we reached Northampton the horses had played up on three occasions, but had been controlled by the whip of the driver. All the while Emily and I were screaming up at him, Father was bellowing at us and Mother, as always, sat observing the pandemonium in silence. And then, when we finally arrived at the centre of town, the rains came down, and not a gentle caressing rain, but torrents, cataracts of water falling from the heavens like a curse; and so great was our desperation not to miss Jenny Lind that we forced ourselves to keep quiet and allow Father to deal with the driver in his own style. Then a bolt of lightning struck the ground close by and the horses refused to move an inch, resolving, moreover, to block the whole street. So finally we opted for continuing on foot, even beneath that unbearable downpour, as far as the Hotel Warner, where we were to be staying that night and, from there, take another carriage with less stupid horses to the church. Our lovely outfits were drenched and sodden, and Father was in an indescribable temper – but there was Jenny, the very Jenny Lind, and all the pains of our odyssey flew from us while she sang and sang, and people ceaselessly threw flowers upon the stage, and she, with her beautiful accent and the tears of emotion welling in her eyes, thanked the kindness of the audience.

When the performance was over we could not stop crying. Emilie lamented that Sue could not have been there with her to share the moment, and I could not stop imagining myself there on the stage, standing weeping under a shower of flowers; and this made us cry all the more, which earned us another reprimand from Father, wholly unaccustomed to public displays of emotion. That evening, beyond Father's thunderstruck reaction to having heard the voice of Jenny Lind, I saw an expression on Mother's face that I cannot recall having seen since then: delight. Mother was smiling, with her head slightly to one side – we were sitting in one of the boxes at the side – utterly absorbed, removed, transfigured by the music. Her eyes were dry, ecstatic, as if she were in a trance – but that smile... By God, I believe that I never again beheld that smile of pleasure so childlike and genuine upon her lips until the day she died, until a few moments before she breathed her final breath. That night I suspected that there was something of Mother in us, that beyond everything else both Emily and I must have something of that woman capable of being so profoundly moved by the music, by a celestial and perfect voice.

For Emilie as much as for me, and perhaps for Austin too, Mother was almost unknown to us in the daily routine. Father was the only member of the family who appeared to understand her, to perceive in her some quality that was never evident to us, something in Mother's distant, respectful and often cold silence. What was it that had tied him so resolutely to a woman like her? Father's determination to make her his wife, no doubt – there was nothing in the world that Father could not achieve if he so desired it. But even so...

After Father's death, on two or three occasions Emilie and I attempted to talk with Mother about it. Three women left alone amongst whom only one had gone through the experience of marriage. While we ate or worked in the garden, or during the sacrosanct hour of sewing, I tried asking her in a jocular way, Emilie asked her as if seeking advice – but it was to no avail. Mother would only reply with a vagueness that made us wonder whether she really remembered Father's presence in her life before they married, or whether, more probably, he had been simply an epistolary figure, a man who would send letters asking her to accompany him as he performed his great work of the world.

II

After the scene of the chipped plate, Austin would ask Emilie whether that day she might perhaps be "in the mood for breaking plates". It became a standard quip of all the family aside from Father. Yet that episode became linked to others that testified and contributed to the separation that was growing between the already divergent paths of Emilie and Father, until finally, despite loving each other – it is inevitable that we love someone as much as we hate them – Emilie and Father drew apart, scarcely uttering a word to each other, and Austin became the mediator in any important situation.

One Sunday Emilie said that at Mount Holyoke, during one of her classes, she had made a casual observation about Lord Jesus; nothing serious, she said. And yet when she said this I could well imagine the tone of what must have come when Emilie had tried to cloak her casual commentary beneath those precise words "nothing serious"; and, indeed, she had been sent to a windowless room to meditate on her wickedness. Maybe she told us this thinking that Father might share her disdain for this unwarranted, and according to her, excessive, punishment. But that morning Father, I suspect, had run up against some weighty problems of his own with regard to his own faith, and as a result his reaction was radically different from that which was hoped for.

"Offences against the Lord are not punished at Mount Holyoke," Father thundered. "Today is the Sabbath, the day of the Church: *that* is where you must go to settle your penurious accounts. Do you not agree?"

Emilie, astonished by Father's support of what she considered plainly and simply to be an outrage, absently commented that Jesus must in truth be fairly nasty to go around causing problems for us, when at the end of the day all we had done was to crucify him, and in the case of her, before she was even born. At this Father turned crimson, Mother pale, and I covered the ears of the pussy cat that had leapt up on my skirt as if seeking shelter. The storm now broke; Father, livid, trying to force her to go to church to repent her sins, Emily refusing, Mother in the middle, tactfully supporting Father, Austin, too distant to help anyone, and I, trying with superhuman force to appear wounded by Emilie's comment – it was my stage of religious enlightenment – when in all honesty it had seemed to me more amusing than anything else. To the church with you! – NO – YES – NO! – until suddenly Emilie leapt up and vanished from our sight. Half an hour went by, then an hour, and as she hadn't reappeared we went to look for her. More time passed, it began to get dark, and the hour of the sermon was fast approaching. Emilie hadn't been seen anywhere, and Father, now concerned although he tried to disguise it, commanded all of us who were left to go with him to church. Mother and I went, all the while bemused as to where on earth the wretched Emilie had hidden, and feeling the wrath of Father upon our own backs. We listened to the sermon with the usual stony expression, while our minds were elsewhere.

At one stage Mother whispered to me:

"Lavinia, you don't think that she could be in the basement, do you?"

"I don't know. When we get back..." I managed to reply before Father or any of the other members of the congregation, inflamed with the panegyric, struck us down with a look that might break the ranks of an army of angels.

Upon leaving the church we hurried directly to the basement to look for her, but it was locked. In the kitchen, Margaret looked down at her feet with an aimless expression, without saying a word, playing the innocent, until Father, suspecting what was by this stage clear for all to see, demanded the key from her. There was Emilie, rocking back and forth on the rocking chair, with her face full of false panic, having compelled Margaret (she said) to lock her in there until the sermon was over.

Father, on the one hand relieved but on the other resolved to punish her, ordered her to lock herself in the
attic until the following day. This Emilie did, but this time
with a genuine and legitimate expression of repentance.
I rightly deserve it, I rightly deserve this cross that I shall
bear, she seemed to be saying with each step that she took
up the curved stairway, seemingly bearing upon her back
the true weight of a cross. In any respect, as far as she was
concerned, the hour of the sermon had indeed passed.

One day a long while after this event, Mattie came to the
Homestead, contrite because her mother had locked her
in the guest bedroom as a punishment for something or
other, and she was now afraid that her mother would love
her no longer. Emilie, beaming from ear to ear, said to her
confidentially:

"Dearest Mattie, no one, and least of all your own mother
who knows us so well, could ever punish a Dickinson by
shutting her up alone. Do not worry, little one, she did it on
purpose. Did you play much while you were up there?"

Mattie, who of course had been playing alone all afternoon, and whose only worry was that the punishment might
mean that her mother no longer loved her, tremulously
answered yes, and Emilie hugged her close and took her to
the kitchen to prepare some of those famous "sighs of the
princess" for tea, which were in reality no more than little
cakes flavoured with cinnamon and ginger.

Emilie's relationship with religion, or better still with religious obligations, was always a point of conflict in our
house. Mother lived in perpetual fearful silence because
of her, I suppose she felt that my sister would go straight
to hell, or that she already was in hell. Austin and I, on the
other hand, tended to yield to the religious customs of the
town, more out of indifference and custom than anything

else, and that way we saved ourselves from the pained reprobation of Mother. Father was different though, he grappled daily with his own incapacity to feel a complete and absolute faith, because, as he himself declared, the great patrimony of faith lay with those who were obtuse, or who were excessively imaginative, and never with those individuals of reason and rationality *in extremis*. And Father was precisely that. Maybe that is the reason that he understood or at least tolerated the intransient, although always intriguing, stance that Emilie would take.

And it certainly wasn't that she didn't believe in God, in a Supreme Being who gave sense and order to the world. On the contrary. Once, when she still spent time outdoors, she told me about her "magic" encounter, which is how she liked to call it at the time. One day, in the back garden of the house, a half-caste woman had appeared. She had probably come up from the South – I'm certain this occurred after the war – she was of an imprecise age, with a body that was still strong. She asked for work, anything would suffice. She said that she had no hopes of ever again seeing any member of her family; she had lost her man during the war through sickness, and from that moment she had made her way alone towards the North, working alternately in the harvests and the mills. Emilie invited her to sit with her in the back veranda and gave her some food. The poor woman was famished, but she was proud and asked for nothing more than work. However, in our house there was scarcely room enough for Maggie and Tom, and merely with them we had more than enough staff. Before resolving anything, Emilie cut bread and cheese, along with a jar of molasses, and brought it all out on a tray to the veranda. My sister worked by her intuition, without deliberation or calculation, but her reflexes were keen and effective in circumstances such as these. While the half-caste woman recounted her misfortunes, Emilie said something along the lines of "I'll pray to God for you". The woman looked at Emilie, but said nothing.

"Do you believe in God?" asked my sister.

"In Santo Domingo there is a black Christ. He was white, but they later painted him black," she replied. "I don't believe in that."

"Do you not believe that Christ is God?"

"I do not believe that there is a God any more *there* than there is anywhere else, ma'am. The rain has a God, the sun has a God, Evil has a God. Duty also. They are all gods who must be obeyed, there is not simply one. And if there were, he wouldn't be in a statue painted black, and neither does your white Christ have any more right to consider himself God."

Later Emilie recounted for me the woman's response with tears in her eyes.

"Do you not see, Vinnie? There is no difference between the way that pagan woman thinks and the way I feel in my heart. God is everywhere aside from where you look for Him. So much determination, so much sacrifice, solemnity and hypocrisy only serve to frighten Him away!"

The visit of that woman also affected me with regard to my stance before God, although in a completely different way. Following their conversation, Emilie begged Austin to find some work for the woman, and he, moved by this, promised her a temporary post in Deerfield, at the house of one of his clients. I hadn't wanted to interrupt Emilie – so struck was I to see her out of her confinement – but as the grateful woman was leaving I stopped her for an instant to give her a little more food. Although she declined, I nevertheless offered her a bag with a couple of pounds of rice and a recently baked loaf of bread. She accepted the bread, but rejected the bag of rice.

"I would have nowhere to cook it, ma'am," she replied simply, and then she left.

I cannot remember ever feeling so ashamed as I did then, so out of place, as if instead of doing her a favour I had actually insulted or mistreated her. How could I not have thought about that, alone as she was, alone on the earth, with neither pot nor pan nor a flame to boil some water? How can one be so dull-witted as to stare misery in the face and not even notice?

At that moment I thought that God, wherever He might be, should not allow people to be so unloved and unprotected as that woman, nor people so heartless, although unintentionally, as me.

III

If Father would upset Emilie with his demands, Mother managed to exasperate her with her obstinate labouring over certain issues. Austin deliberately paid no heed to Mother's orders, while I opted for evading them, offering myself with theatrical obsequiousness to run any errand and perform whichever chore would take me away from the house by at least two hundred yards. Austin would call me *the deserter*, although I suspect that the term in reality originated from my sister. She, generally in the house, had little option but to battle with Mother, sometimes with good humour, sometimes with patience, and sometimes, like the time the Hollands visited us unannounced from Northampton, with cries fit to raise heaven. One night Dr and Mrs Holland appeared in Amherst with the expressed intention of spending the night at our house. They had spent the last six hours riding in a carriage drawn by exhausted horses, along muddy and slippery roads in the midst of a frightful fog. Mother, as she always did when something took her by surprise, reacted with excessive kindness, almost with the same servile disposition that I offered myself to run her errands.

"Doctor Holland, would you care for another cup of tea? Perhaps with a little more honey? A glass of sherry, Mrs Holland? The bedroom of the first floor has been prepared, would you like to go up? Would you like some slippers, perhaps? Shall I have more wood placed in the fire?"

In this way, with an exasperating insistency, she carried on for more than an hour.

Mother was not normally like this, usually quite the opposite, but she would sometimes react in such a way to certain situations, like this for example, when her hospitality was under the keen, albeit indifferent scrutiny of Father, something we could never understand. Until finally, after hours of ridiculous offerings of this and that, and when I was just preparing to escape to the basement, Emilie, exasperated by this insistent pressure, blurted out·

"And would you like me to say my prayers out loud? Or perhaps you would care for me to recite the Declaration of Independence, Dr Holland? Surely you would delight in hearing the Ten Commandments? Or examining my needlework, perhaps?"

Just like the episode of the chipped plate, this passed into the annals of our family history. For years Austin would plead Emilie, mocking Mother all the while even in front of her, kindly to recite the Declaration of Independence. Mother would end up laughing at the joke, although at that time she was far from amused, and her dealings with Emilie grew more distant, almost cold, for several weeks.

4

How We Survived Love, among Other Things

How do I love thee? Let me count the ways...
— E. Browning

I

*I*n the winter of 1855, aside from Austin, the whole family went to Washington.

It was the second time that I went to that city in the company of Father. The first, some years before, Mother and I had gone while Emilie offered to stay at home with Sue, both of them dying of fright every night but earnestly believing in their role as watchers of the palace.

Father dedicated his time to politics at Congress, while we wandered leisurely through the unfamiliar streets, in my case in the occasional company of other ladies. Emilie preferred her long walks inside the hotel, chatting about this and that with whomsoever struck her as being exotic, which caused Mother to ask herself repeatedly why on earth Father had taken it into his head to take us all along with him. I remember in particular a certain Mr Elliot, of New Bedford, who was lodging at the Hotel Willard and who also went along to the sessions at Congress, and had likewise brought along to Washington his wife and daughters. I remember him in particular because every night he would kiss his daughters on the cheek, two kisses each, wishing them sweet dreams, and then, furtively, he

would kiss his wife on the corner of the mouth, feigning
a formal gesture that eventually made her blush and both
of them laugh. That was how I noticed that Father had
never kissed us, not once in all his years, not even to bid
us goodnight. Never. He would have given his life for
us, but at the same time he would have done so without
telling us that he was doing so. Is that not curious? By
which I mean, curious to realize that something that you
have taken for being normal, or at least habitual, may not
be normal.

Neither do I remember Father ever kissing Mother, for
example, but I do remember him embracing Austin each
time that he was leaving for Cambridge.

Such a discovery, however, did not make me hate Father,
but it did make me admire Mr Elliot in an uncommon way,
wishing with all my heart to be one day a woman such as
his wife who would blush beneath a secret and compliant
kiss.

Those frosty days took place amidst sombre afternoon
gatherings at the hotel, formal strolls in the streets, and
an excursion to the tomb of General Washington on
Mount Vernon, and other equally festive celebrations.
Emilie declared herself ill for most of the time, although
I suspect that she played up this role so as to avoid the
social gatherings and the balls that so bored her and so
delighted me. She would shut herself in her room to
write letters, and this became her activity day and night.
Not so for me – I had gone to Washington with the secret
intention of ridding my thoughts of Joseph, who those days
was planning his marriage to the ineffable and charming
Laura Baker. I would willingly have taken myself to Alaska
to marry an Eskimo, but Washington was nearer and far
more entertaining.

Mother, Emilie and I spent the entire two weeks leading up to going to Washington sewing our dresses and fixing our outfits as best we could. Emilie was not a good seamstress; she was bad on purpose, just as she was terrible at cleaning, simply because she disliked both tasks. "I prefer pestilence", she would say, and, with similar predisposition, "I prefer to wear rags!" In the face of such an attitude it always seemed easier simply to relieve her of these activities, even though this entailed doubling the burden upon ourselves.

Washington was for us a very beautiful city: flourishing, modern, clean, and without those dark and gloomy tenements that sheltered the indigents from all over the world, such as they say fill New York. Washington was more like a city predestined to be the head of the Nation, with gentle suburbs and majestic avenues, graceful buildings of immaculate marble and European details at the corners. The ladies, even on a daily basis, wore pointed bonnets adorned with lace, feathers, flowers and ribbons, while the rest of their outfits could include cotton or velvet collars, cuffs embroidered even with pearls, veils of elaborate muslin, beautifully tailored riding jackets, leather and satin ballerina shoes that were braided at the ankles; and for festive occasions, bustiers tightened at the back with puffed sleeves to the elbow and ample straight necklines that revealed the thrust of the chest. And there were we, with our rudimentary and passé frocks made of percale, and the oriental luxury of three pleats at our chest, our plain bonnets and, above all, our dreary travelling overcoats with an occasional chequered shawl over our shoulders... How, in the name of God, were we to receive any admiring looks, save merely charitable or astonished glances?

May God forgive me for invoking His name in such vulgar and mundane rhetoric, but, as Sue would so rightly say, the only capital that we "New Englanders" could boast of was the capital of vitality. To be lively and humble, unlike the young ladies of Washington or even those of Northampton, who, in the eyes of us enforced puritans, seemed to emulate the very fashion of Paris or London, with their wide six-dollar hats bought at Mrs Osborne's, their pale shawls of either oriental silk or merino wool from Stoddard & Lathrops.

When Father decided to remain in the city longer than originally planned, and Mother expressed her intention to return to Amherst at once, I begged Emilie to accompany me to Philadelphia to visit Eliza Coleman. A few years previously cousin Olivia had died, and since then, cousin Eliza had languished in her room, prisoner to a dreadful and incurable melancholy. Of course, I had to appeal to every manner of concession, entreaty, offer and promise in order to convince my sister, bored by now of the hotel and eager to get back to Sue, her soul-mate, to agree to continue the trip for a while longer. At last we went, something that Emilie would thank me for for the rest of her life, because there, in Philadelphia, not only did she discover the un-conditional love of the Coleman family, but she also met the man who would become, from then onwards, almost her confessor: Reverend Charles Wadsworth.

Wadsworth was well-known throughout the whole of the north-east of the country for his dazzling sermons, even those in the West Coast had begun to hear of him, and he would constantly receive invitations to give talks and seminars. Emilie could well have recognized him from his name alone, but perhaps not; but the first time we went to hear one of the Reverend's sermons her eyes lit up with the illumination of a genuine discovery. Enraptured, she decided to write him a letter there and then so as to inform him of her admiration, and to discuss certain issues with him – Emilie was always discussing the more obscure elements of the Doctrine – and the Reverend replied to her letter forthwith, stunned, I would imagine, by the sinuous but withal sharp wit and style of my sister. Following this brief exchange of letters we went once again, and for the final time, to hear one of his sermons. Emilie, from the pew, gazed spellbound, ecstatically, at the indisputable skill with which the Reverend delivered his oratory; and he, from the pulpit, surely scanned the congregation in vain to identify his rare epistolary friend.

They did not meet then, neither did they see each other face to face – nobody introduced them – of that I am certain. However, this interchange did indeed continue, until one day the Reverend, as he was passing through Amherst, came to visit her. Wadsworth was not only married, but he also appeared to adore his wife, so much so that had Emilie really felt that blinding love that everyone now believes, she would have understood that it was to be an unfulfilled love from the beginning, fated to fulfil itself over time through the contact of paper and ink. As for me, I know that they never met at that early stage, and that when they did effectively meet, the years had hewn him into a sensitive yet firm man, devoted to teaching and to his family, and my sister into a *rara avis* who from long before, far too long perhaps, preferred the solitude of her books and the perfect relationships of letters to personal meetings.

They remained friends until he died. He was her confessor in more than one sense, her unconditional ally in all matters of the spirit. I cannot believe that any other person lived whom Emilie could confide in so deeply, aside from Sue.

Years later, and only because the Reverend had been dead now some time and could no longer affect her with his commentaries, the inside members of our family, myself included, were compelled to bid our silence as rumours circulated concerning the "amorous" motives of Emilie's reclusion.

II

Next after the poor Reverend on the long list of people who encouraged the extravagant ways of my sister was Colonel Thomas Wentworth Higginson, who today figures as the principal editor and "inveterate admirer" of the works of my sister. I cannot blame him entirely for this: I myself have been to a large degree responsible for much of what happened. But that is another story that I'd rather not talk about at the moment.

The first of the many meetings with Colonel Higginson took place in this house, which is where most things took place in Emily's life and also my own; and from my modest vantage point as spy, that meeting has to be the most memorable spectacle put on by Emilie that I can remember.

The Colonel and the Massachusetts regiments had been posted to South Carolina. From the moment that Emilie started writing letters to him – letters to a man preparing for or even fighting a war – which at the beginning were not even signed, she asked him to come and visit Amherst. I have only seen two of these letters, but this has been enough for me to form this opinion. He, for his part, asked her to visit him in Boston, but Emilie invariably made up excuses, such as declaring that Father would not allow her to make such a journey. Such an excuse in my eyes could not have been valid: I myself had been to Boston on various occasions with the exclusive purpose of buying some fabric, or a certain bonnet, and I cannot see why she could not have gone with the same purpose. But no, there was always something: some minor illness, a persistent cough, the winter weather, the terrible state of the roads, the bereavement of losing someone close, the inevitable need to do Father's bidding. Could perhaps you not come to Amherst, Colonel, to this town of shadows where I am queen?

Before the war reached its conclusion, Higginson was relieved of his military responsibilities; he returned wounded but at least in one piece, nothing too terrible when compared with other far more irreparable mutilations. He decided to settle in Newport to devote himself entirely to literature, whilst others, like Hawthorne, were abandoning it. Emilie herself sent him notice of the death of Mr Hawthorne, when Higginson was on the point of returning to the South.

The years passed, the war ended and yet the letters continued to flow. I am talking in terms of many years. Then, at the turn of the 1860s, Sam Bowles – my dear friend Sam, always so precise – started to call Emilie "the Queen Recluse". Emilie, without doubt, had by this stage begun to forge that identity for herself; as slowly, very slowly, like a bee slowly building its comb of perfect hexagons, she had begun to create herself from the outside inwards, closing behind her all the doors, bricking up the entrances to her interior, to the Queen inside, in such a way that now she could only devote herself to that for which she had in truth been born.

Yes, I am talking of the passage of years. Emilie never went to Boston, nor to Newport, at least not to see the Colonel, but even so she would implore him ever more vehemently to be the one to pay her a visit. Hawthorne's death came and went; Mr Emerson was in Amherst for a little over a month in order to give a series of seminars at the College. But Emilie, although Emerson was a guest on more than one occasion at the house of Austin and Sue, did not participate in any of these soirées. I mentioned to her once, just as Father, Mother and Sue also warned her, that she would never again have such an opportunity as that. But Emilie, with an indifference that seemed to me somewhat affected, maintained that Emerson's book of poems was far more valuable to her than his presence, and that anyway, he would no doubt intimidate her to such a degree that the meeting would turn hostile.

Ralph Waldo Emerson therefore passed through Amherst, and as we had predicted, never returned. Soon after, Carlo, the dog that Emilie loved so much, died. I remember this because at that stage, all of a sudden, I realized that I was thirty years old and that not only for my sister, but also for myself, fates had been decided, like it or not. Destiny had isolated all of us save Emilie, who had spun for herself that inexorable chrysalis, sealed off and protected, or at least more so than ours. Because ours was a shared destiny, the destiny of men, of chance, perhaps even of God. Emilie's was not.

Finally, in 1870, Higginson appeared in Amherst, en route for Philadelphia or somewhere, according to what he said. He had, of course, given a month's notice in writing of his visitation, as was the custom in those days; and Emilie, of course, spent the whole morning charging about the kitchen with cookies and loaves of bread of sufficient quantity to feed a starving army. Both Mother and Father let her be, knowing full well who the afternoon visitor was, and they set off at midday to Belchertown.

At precisely the designated hour he arrived. I was in the kitchen preparing the final things. Emilie had put on a simple white dress and had brushed her hair as always, but perhaps this time a little more carefully – her coppery hair thoroughly combed, rather severely parted in the middle and held up in a netted bun – with a shawl about her shoulders and nothing more. When the Colonel arrived Emilie was in the garden picking water lilies. I frantically waved to her from the kitchen, and yet the front door was not opened until she was inside, waiting for him in the parlour, like an actress would await the rising of the curtain to begin her soliloquy.

The Colonel was a tall man, of noble and distinguished bearing, and he walked with a slight limp that could as well have been natural as a product of the war. He had nothing in his hands save his hat, and he crossed the parlour with wide steps, stopping to observe the piano. As he drew his hand along the polished surface of the piano lid, Emilie appeared from the shadows like a red-haired, pale-faced ghost, clutching the water lilies in her hand, and walked up to him. I remember that what most struck me – I was spying from the corridor – was the voice of my sister. She was not speaking in her normal voice, which was normally low in tone, a little hoarse but agreeable, if indeed not particularly feminine. No, on this occasion she was speaking in the tone of a small child, breathing sharply and shallowly, barely whispering the words.

"These are my introduction," she said, placing the flowers in the Colonel's hands.

I would have given my life to have seen his face at this, but his back was to me. What I do remember, however, was that he gave a start. What could he have been expecting exactly?

"Emily!" exclaimed the Colonel, somewhat taken aback. But he quickly recovered, and gave a brief bow. "Miss Dickinson, I am at your service."

"Forgive me if I appear frightened," Emilie continued in that voice that was in reality her voice of panic. "It is only that I rarely talk to strangers. Indeed I rarely even leave this house, and when I do find myself in the presence of those whom I do not know, I never know exactly what to say."

"Ah, but I should not be considered a stranger to you, Miss Dickinson," the Colonel said in an affable and amused tone.

"Emily," she said, "just Emily."

"As you wish."

They then sat beside the piano, to my great disappointment, as from that angle it was all too easy for them to assess whether I was coming or going. As a result I had to abandon the idea of surreptitiously witnessing the entire encounter.

"Finally I have the pleasure of meeting you," said the Colonel, perhaps a little abruptly owing to the unusual position in which he found himself seated for conversation.

"Incredible things never surprise me. Do they surprise you?"

"Do they *not* surprise you?"

"It is simply that they shouldn't be surprising. That's incredible, is it not? How have you found Amherst? Have you seen anything of this vast area, Colonel? The mountains, perhaps? Have you seen the late summer flowers in the valley?"

"Very little, if I must be honest, and less than I should have wished. In any respect I have tomorrow. Perhaps you would like to accompany me on a walk around the surrounding area?"

"It would be a privilege, but, as I said earlier, I rarely leave this house. Consider the house like my castle, my sacred enclosure: I live within; I have the piano, my books, my room upstairs, right there above your head. I have all that I can see from the window, which is almost the whole world, or at least almost all the world that exists, along with the world that is revealed within the pages of my books. Does this perhaps seem curious to you?"

"Curious is a good word... Have you never felt any want of employment, of going off the grounds, of visiting other parts of the world that you cannot see from your window, or of receiving a visitor?"

"I never thought of conceiving that I could ever have the slightest approach to such a want in all future time. For me, Colonel, I find ecstasy in living – the mere sense of living is joy enough."

From my wretched hideaway, I sensed that the conversation was a particular design of Emilie's to rid herself of the fear she was suffering; the fear that I could sense trembling through her skin, quivering in her voice. Very carefully, therefore, I slipped away towards the stairway, and thence to the kitchen to prepare the tray of still warm cookies.

I allowed some time to pass before interrupting them with the tray and the evening's aperitif. It was then that I heard Emilie declare that she had never had a mother, and I thanked the heavens that Mother was not present – nor Father, for that matter – and in spite of seeing some truth in what she said, I realized that there was and always would be a side of my sister to which I would never gain access. Of course, time and life soften this type of certainty, and as I recall that feeling and that episode once again, I deem that in truth I knew it from long before, when it was already too late.

And so I entered the parlour with the tray. The Colonel rose to his feet to greet me and to take the tray from my hands. Emilie, now far more composed, gazed at me without seeing me. The Colonel, on the other hand, seemed troubled, unable to decide whether to sit once again, to move seats, or to include me in the conversation – a project that I swiftly dispelled with my intention to return to my secret observation point by the stairs – or whether simply to go. Over an hour had passed by this stage.

"And people must have puddings," Emilie said while I was still with them, trying to explain to our guest that the cookies were one of Emilie's specialities, and that Father could survive on only those cookies and the bread that she prepared.

The Colonel was watching her, astonished, and I made out as if nobody had said anything. Emilie was talking now about cakes, and she began to recite the recipe for ginger-bread:

One quart flour, 1/2 cup butter, 1/2 cup cream, one tablespoon ground ginger, one teaspoon soda, one teaspoon salt, make up with good molasses.

"I thank you for this kind gesture, Miss Lavinia," he said, trying to maintain some sense of civility, and, I imagine, some sense of coherence.

"Oh but you must say that to my sister, Colonel," I replied somewhat sardonically. "It was she who baked them early this morning."

"They are my duty," Emilie stated simply. "Poetry is my duty. A word of a verse, a piece of ginger to regulate the acidity of bread, a sonnet read in a hushed voice, warm molasses for the gingerbread mix. These are all my duties."

Higginson recuperated sufficiently upon hearing the magic word.

"And how would you know that something that you had read was poetry? Tell me that. How would you know that it was poetry?"

Emilie took one of the cookies and broke it roughly, as a greedy young girl would have done, while she dwelt upon this question. She then placed both pieces back on the tray.

"If I read a book and it makes my whole body so cold no fire can ever warm me," she replied, "I know *that* is poetry. If I feel physically as if the top of my head were taken off, I know that is poetry. These are the only ways I know it. Is there any other way?"

I retired from the room when I heard the Colonel mutter some response, but he was evidently highly perturbed. Soon after this he left. I could see him from the window walking briskly towards the carriage, no longer holding himself upright, gallant and noble, as he had when he arrived, but hunched up, seeming drained and exhausted.

Emilie, seated at the piano, radiant, began to play the *Pathétique* of Beethoven with a skill that I had not expected, as if some hidden source of energy had suddenly revitalised her; and at last she unfastened the net that held up her hair bun and said:

"Vin, this is the most important day of my life."

I could scarcely do more than smile, without understanding how on earth she had managed, in such a short time, to reverse their roles. When a magnolia blooms, it's as if the rest of the tree falls into the shadow, as if all the green simply disappears into the heart of that hermetic whiteness that is a magnolia flower, unique amongst flowers. In that very same way Emilie had sucked the Colonel's energy in the matter of a couple of hours, until he withered and she bloomed.

The Colonel was well-known in the select circles of literature, and he continued to be so until the day of his death, I suspect, although I remain to be convinced that such recognition was entirely deserved. He was more of a political animal, cultured, sombre and imposing, yet at the same time alert and persuasive, as only those naturally gifted individuals *can* be, or those who affect an excessive concern for others. In the case of the Colonel, Emilie and I could never reach an agreement. She considered him her saviour, rescuer, instructor, master and critic. She tried through all her means to humble herself to the position of disciple. Such a paradox! Emilie, the disciple of the Colonel. Who could learn more from the other? I'm not sure, but I believe that she knew full well, despite that role of pupil that she had assumed so obediently.

I myself maintained an unfaltering attitude and conduct towards him while Emilie was still unknown. This was mainly due to her, and to the strange dependence that she had on him, strange because she never really needed him. My sister needed nobody for her writing. She needed no external influence beyond silence and solitude, a few pencils, her bedroom, sun-lit by day, candle-lit by night. Night-time was when she really worked. That was all, I swear. Maybe she would have needed him in order to be published. Yes, I feel that in essence *this* was what it was all about, although she, of course, would be the last to admit it.

Only a short while ago we found out through certain channels that are not relevant to this account that Helen Hunt Jackson paid more than five hundred dollars to put together a personal edition of a small volume of Emily's poetry. Five hundred dollars is an extraordinary sum of money, by any standards. The same quantity as Father's contribution to the war effort through Austin, who never enlisted. But is it really such an extraordinary sum? Why didn't we, the Dickinsons, pay for an edition for Emilie? Could we perhaps not have afforded it?

Well, that cannot be the case. If we could contribute to a war, we certainly could have contributed far more to art – indeed to that which lies beyond art: Emilie's happiness. Father had also donated money, for example, to cover the financial deficit of the church: fifty dollars for Emilie and myself, two hundred and fifty for he and Mother. Money also for the railroad, money for the thoroughbred horses that were always his pride and joy, money for a lunatic asylum, for Amherst College, money for Austin's house...

Could we really not have helped Emilie publish her poems while she was alive, while we all knew that she still considered it a possibility, while all of us members of the family had praised her few poems published anonymously in the *Springfield Republican* thanks to the modest efforts of Sam Bowles? In reality what difference would five hundred miserable dollars have made alongside the possibility of allowing my sister to enjoy some recognition in her life?

Maybe if we had offered she would have declined, that's almost certain, but even so I still cannot fathom why we never did offer. It is now my duty to redress that error, and I am content to do so, and I do not care how much is at stake: the Dickinson inheritance is mine, and nobody beyond Mattie is still living. This work for Emilie is the only thing that I deem worthy; five hundred dollars, a thousand dollars would mean nothing. Nothing will absolve us of the guilt of not having acted when we had the chance.

III

Soon after Emilie's funeral, a neighbour from Amherst, whose name I choose not to recall and least of all repeat, asked me straight out, following a curt exchange of words about an unrelated matter, if it was true that the thwarted love of my sister had been Reverend Wadsworth, also deceased by then – thankfully, I might add, because the Reverend not only had been married but moreover took gossip about his life very badly. Mrs F. had certainly never been a friend of the family, and I felt no obligation

whatsoever to reply to such an impertinent and out of
place question. Nevertheless I gave her an answer, saying
yes to her question. Her jaw dropped in astonishment upon hearing this and, unable to close her mouth through
the use of her own muscles, she covered her mouth with
her gloved hand. What answer could this wretched woman
have been expecting? Without delay I assumed my most
elementary confidential tone and whispered to her ear that
she must not, "under any circumstance", repeat this to
anybody, full knowing that in a matter of hours the news
would have spread throughout town like a mudslide in the
mountains in spring.

And that is effectively what happened. There is not a soul
in Amherst who does not doubt that my sister enclosed
herself for ever within the walls of this house owing to
lovesickness, and that the perpetrator of such an ailment
should be none other than Reverend Wadsworth of Philadelphia, whom Emilie had seen only as many times
as you could count on the fingers of one hand. Charles
Wadsworth, in a word, was the perfect and emblematic
love that could never be: married when he met Emilie,
vehement, known the country over for his speeches and
sermons about almost any subject, educated at the best
colleges, frugal, with that hint of enigmatic disdain for the
daily trappings of life that endowed him with that strange
aura of being a man "unable to resolve even the problem
of his own existence". That one element was enough to
fascinate my sister disproportionately.

Emilie, as I have said, had a special predilection for eloquent men, and Reverend Wadsworth was precisely that,
no doubt about it. He was eloquent right up to the day of
his death, and just as he was eloquent in his life, so he was
in his letters; of that I am certain. Perhaps it is true that
Emilie may have felt something beyond admiration for

him, but if the truth be told, Emilie never experienced any love more real than that of Judge Phillip Otis Lord. *His* was the love that lit up the final years of her life – *his* was the love that I, amongst many others, strove to discourage.

There was no way that this love would not crystallize, in an almost physical way, I would say, from such stagnant and fruitless beginnings into the single most precious jewel that my sister bore with her to the grave.

It is a love story by no means spectacular, beyond the issue of the Judge's age, which was almost twice that of Emilie's. In fact, Otis Lord had been a school companion of Father's; they had attended the same college together and had taken the same law courses. Father admired him greatly, and indeed, he was a man to be admired: his broad knowledge and learning, his power of oratory, his resolute will. But he was also one whom you might laugh at in secret, behind his back, for his extraordinary affectations and his tremendous, almost grotesque, grandiloquence. Nothing made me happier than mimicking Judge Lord, obviously when Father, and then later Emilie, were absent.

What's more, this love story, despite containing nothing more exciting than radically differing ages, could never have taken place during Father's lifetime, much less during the lifetime of Lord's wife, Elizabeth. When Father died, the Judge was an indispensable source of solace for all of us, besides being the one who instructed us through the legal pathways of the family estate. But he could never have been anything more than this, and if earlier there had been any intrigue, Emilie was careful in never telling a soul, not even Sue. Two years later, Elizabeth died, and *that* was when things changed.

I myself knew, principally because I was the one who personally took the letters into town, that Emilie was writing letters and sending them to an outlandish address that bore as its subject the name of a shipbuilding company in Salem. That was where Lord lived in an enormous mansion with his sister-in-law, Mary Farley, and her daughter, Abbey, who had taken the responsibility of arranging the affairs of the Judge's life. They were the first to oppose the idea of an alleged *affaire*, and they were quick to make this contrary opinion public. I suspect that the Judge himself was not too bothered by this; he was not a man to pay much heed to the opinion of others, at least not in regard to opinions regarding his own private life.

Soon after the death of his wife, Lord appeared all of a sudden in Amherst. He had come to take Emilie away to live with him. I cannot bear to remember that afternoon, nor the secret meeting that he conducted with my sister in the library, with the door closed, nor the trembling expression of happiness and fear in Emilie's face when she came into the kitchen to tell me about what I had already imagined a while before. No – now, just as then, I would rather not think about it. I ran as fast as I was able, in desperation, to Austin's house, hammered on the door with all my strength until Sue, terrified, opened the door and I collapsed at her feet, my legs unable to support me. I told her that Lord had come to take Emilie away, and that she was in agreement. That they would be leaving in a matter of a couple of days. I could talk no longer.

Sue, I remember perfectly, ordered me to stand up, and grasping me firmly by the shoulders as you would a child said:

"Lavinia, Emily will not go with him. Not with that gentleman... ridiculous. It is too late, and she knows that."

"Oh she may know it, but she no longer cares," I protested.

"It will not happen," she said, and headed off towards the Homestead.

I never knew what Sue and my sister discussed, nor whether Lord took part in the discussion, although it is likely that he did, judging by the way I saw him later from afar, dishevelled and furious, walking to his carriage like an ill-fated hunter, beating the bushes with his cane. I never found out what they talked about, but I do know that I am responsible, as much as is Sue, for Emilie not going with him on that occasion.

When Sue returned from the Homestead I was sitting waiting for her in the parlour, expecting to hear the worst from her mouth: that my sister was resolved to go, that despite his anger he would return for her in any case, if not this week then in a month or even more. What would a question of time matter if she were going? To my surprise Sue did not say this. She asked me to return home as Emilie needed me, and that I need not worry about Lord. I asked her if Emilie was going, and she answered:

"Emilie knows what she has to do. Perhaps she does not want to accept it yet, but she knows what to do."

However, despite Sue's convictions, the idea of marrying the Judge did not disappear; quite the contrary. From that fateful afternoon the letters continued to flow between them with ever greater frequency, only now I was not the one to post them, but Tom, the Irish gardener whom Emilie so liked. The letters were addressed directly to Lord, no longer to the fictitious address of before. From that moment on we made no mention of the subject with her, nor did I talk of the matter with Sue, tacitly deciding to await the next move, certain that Lord would tire of fighting on all sides, and that my sister would return to her senses. It was, however, luck that assisted us in our selfish wishes. Soon after, Lord suffered a stroke while at home in Salem. As he was a well-known figure throughout the state, the news was immediately published in the following day's *Springfield Republican*, which no sooner had I read than I hurried up to my sister's room. I knew that she would not have picked up the newspaper by then, as I was always the first to read it, then Ned or Mattie if they were at home that day, Emilie always receiving it around dusk. Ah, with what sinister joy did I show her that piece of news! Emilie smiled as she took the newspaper, wholly unsuspecting, but then in an instant turned pale and stiff like a wax statue, so much so that I thought she would faint. Tom, who had found out about the news, had followed me upstairs, and for the first time in his life he entered Emilie's room without knocking, saying as he did: "I thought of you straight away. I'm so terribly sorry." As if coming to life with a dreadful cry, Emilie hurled herself against Tom's chest, and he held her there, in such an honest and forthright embrace of consolation and comfort that my miserable joy vanished at once.

I tore up the newspaper, disgusted at my spitefulness, but it was now too late to worry about myself.

At times I think about the viciousness that drove me to wound Emilie in that way. Incomprehensible acts. I loved her with all my heart, I needed her close to me in order to defend her, even though I knew her to be strong in her extravagances, to care for her, because caring for her was as much part of my being as it was my role. It has always been my role in the family – defend. Defend with the ferocity of Saul filled with the Holy Spirit, defend and protect. Emilie, more than anyone else in this world, needed me and the protective shell that I held around her – protected from visitors, from engagements, from errands and chores, from social and even family obligations, protected from economic worries, (women, Father would say, should remain free from all forms of debt), free to do what she wished with her time.

It is for that reason that now, without her, my life has little sense.

Without her I am a useless army.

I cannot imagine that this could justify the wicked way I have behaved sometimes, or maybe the justification lies in the fact that Father always considered her a Dickinson, just as he did Austin, whilst I was always... I was always a sort of frivolous daughter – little Vinnie with her low-cut dresses, her suitors and her ridiculous songs.

One afternoon – we would have been about twenty at the time – we had an argument. Father had gone to Boston to visit Austin, and he had returned with *The Letters of Abelard and Héloïse*, and also with a wrap of satin and some velvet ribbons that Austin had found in a store and had bought for us, although I'm certain he was thinking about me when he bought them as I was always begging him for such things. I was never a great reader, at least not like my sister, but I derived great pleasure from reading, and the *Historia calamitatum*, as everyone knew the work, was the most daring and passionate thing we could read at that time. Although Father had announced that he would be the first to read it, the pair of us pounced upon the book, Emilie, the quicker, grabbing it first.

"Sorry Vin, it's mine."

"Why?" I protested. "Father brought it for nobody in particular."

"But I'm the eldest," she replied absently, opening the book before my eyes with every intention of starting it there and then. When Emilie did these things I wanted to hit her.

"So I'm the youngest. So what? I'll swap it for all the other stuff," I offered. I did so want to read that book.

Emilie lifted her eyes from the page, took the satin between her hands and wrapped the ribbons around it like one might truss a stuffed turkey.

"I wouldn't know what to do with it, Vin."

"You could make yourself a new dress...'

"You too – and you would put it to much better use."

"But that's not fair. I'm not interested in fabrics."

"Not interested in fabrics? Since when?" Emilie asked, mockingly, as she sat at the dining table and took out of her box some pieces of paper and a pencil. She would always take notes while she read, but that also meant that she was ready to begin reading – that the conversation was over.

I went out into the garden nearly crying with rage. Why was she doing this to me? Why must she, in addition to Father and Austin, make me feel like some silly little doll, incapable of anything more than choosing a nice bonnet or mimicking others peoples' gestures like a monkey? I could tolerate it from Austin, well, I had no choice really; indeed at times I even enjoyed acting frivolously, putting him in impossible situations, like when I obliged him to accompany me to the Boston stores and to parties "of foolish girls". But that was Austin. With Emilie it was different, or that's what I believed: she knew more about me than I of her, and in that precise moment I considered her the same as Austin, arrogant and pedantic, and whom I had no choice, of course, but to love with a certain distance.

When I returned to the house, resolved to bring up not simply the subject of the book but all those things that I felt needed to be said to make it clear *who* I was, Emilie was reading in her armchair, utterly absorbed, jotting down things on the paper without even appearing to look at it. She hadn't even heard me enter. But what could she be absorbed in? What did she know of love? Nothing, absolutely nothing. Nothing beyond what she could read or what she could be told, nothing more than the secret and vague hope on her rides with Emmons. She knew nothing of love, and neither she nor anybody else had the right to judge me in that way.

It was that very afternoon that I told Emilie about what had happened with Joseph in the maple forest. I told her crudely, vulgarly, more to hurt her than to share my experiences with her. I recounted details that had never actually occurred so as not to reduce the story to a single and simple sentence: Joseph and I had made love. Or something similar.

Emily had stopped reading, and she now was looking at me in her strange way, without seeing me, or perhaps gazing past me at something in the garden. She said nothing, not a word, and when I finished, she lowered her head, took the pen once again and dipped it in the ink as if she were about to write. About what I had told her, perhaps? I wasn't even aware whether she had heard me fully or not; Emilie could be impenetrable, sealed, as only a Dickinson can be. She was also capable of closing the compartments of her mind at will, and to isolate her thoughts, while her eyes gazed out as if lost, eyelids half-closed. With people who were not family, she was even capable of showing surprise or disapproval, muttering the occasional word that would allow the speaker, although secretly being ignored, to persist in the illusion of being politely listened to.

Well, if Emilie could be impenetrable, so could I. On that occasion I likewise said nothing, and just as I had entered, so I left. That lack of response let me know that my mission was accomplished, that my selfish soul had achieved its aims, and, moreover, that I was now alone with my secret. Because in all honesty I had shared absolutely nothing with my sister. You might even say that I had thrown it in her face: I was a woman and she was not. I knew about love, and she knew only what Héloïse chose to tell her from the twelfth century.

My sister, as I mentioned, said not one word, and if what happened later had not happened, I would have sworn that Emilie simply scrubbed it from her mind, that is if any of my words about the *affaire* in the woods ever made it as far as her mind. But nearly thirty years later, when marriage to the Judge seemed a foregone conclusion, she brought up the subject as if it were a mere trifle.

We were in the kitchen, I feeding my pussy cats, she about to make a loaf of bread. Suddenly something appeared to bother her – those sudden anxieties of hers were common, appearing as if out of a dream. I knew something bothered her as she was talking about something that had happened to Samuel Bowles years before, and she stopped mid-sentence.

"Vin," she said.

"Hmm?"

"Intercourse. Does it hurt?"

I tried to recall whether there had been any pain, but, as I've said, my memory is an untidy and arbitrary place. If there had been any pain, there was no trace of it left upon my body.

"No," I replied.

"Hmmm," said Emilie, and carried on mixing lard with flour for the bread, while I went to the garden as if I had something very urgent to see to in the snow.

IV

> Much madness is divinest sense
> To a discerning eye;
> Much sense the starkest madness.
> ...Assent, and you are sane;
> Demur, you're straightway dangerous,
> And handled with a chain.
>   – E. Dickinson

Emilie had gone to Boston for a number of months, roughly April to November, to have problems with her eyesight dealt with. Doctor Willard Williams was seeing her in his surgery religiously three times a week, and all the while Emilie was suffering exile, the inability to read or write anything, in the company of our cousins Fanny and Loo, who did their utmost to attend to her and to amuse her. However, although Emilie would always thank them with a radiant smile for their efforts, in June I received a very brief letter from her telling me that she felt "as in de Quincey's London before taking opium, like the prisoner of Chillon, chained in his private darkness, at the mercy of spiders, rats, and tombs. Why would the poor prisoner want to regain his liberty, if outside the walls of the cell there is nothing left for him save the burning sun? Pay no attention to me, Vinnie, this incapacity of mine does have some good in it. It has made me think that if I never regain the use of my eyes, there are so few genuinely decent books in the world that I'd soon find someone to read them all to me."

I may have considered, on more than one occasion, that Emilie was disturbed in an essentially irreparable way. Austin may have thought the same, although he had too much respect for her intellect, as did Sue, to consider this seriously. In any case, and I stand by what I say, Austin and Sue would only think of her eccentricities as "poses".

Was Emilie really different? Well, to tell the truth, all of us Dickinsons were, and remain so to this day. We all carry in our veins the unruly blood of old Grandfather Samuel. Each one of us, in our own way, has always felt more comfortable amongst ourselves than amongst others; and for that reason when they now speak of reclusion, isolation, daughters carrying out their father's decree of not marrying, quite frankly I find it quite amusing. Whatever the situation was, Emilie certainly *felt* different. The day she turned eighteen she said to me.

"Vin. I am no longer seventeen."

I looked at her, somewhat baffled.

"And?..."

"Well, I shall not be pretty. This mouth, these gypsy eyes. They will be with me for ever."

I then remembered how much she had played with the idea of transforming herself into the Belle of Amherst. Some odd desire, probably based in those literary characters who avowed it, had convinced her that such a transformation would occur magically between the age of fifteen and seventeen. Therefore, when she looked at herself in the mirror that day and saw the same large and slightly childlike eyes as always – I mean – when she realized that her physical features, just like mine, just like everyone's, had not changed from one day to the next and were not likely to change in the future, she decided that the fantasy of beauty was over. She no longer had any need for the Belle of Amherst. I cannot recall her suffering too much over this, nor do I recall having detected in her tone anything other than a touch of resignation, as if she had always secretly suspected the truth. At that moment I felt more beautiful than Emilie; I knew that my looks were gracious, my nose delicate, my hair darker and more abundant, and if I let Emilie know this, when carried away by adolescent arrogance, she would invariably find some way to make me feel comical and silly.

With respect to our parents, I can only recall one occasion, despite it being when we were very young, in which I perceived that Father likewise did not consider Emilie entirely normal. Father and I, and perhaps Austin too, were looking at the snow. One of those afternoons in which there is nothing to do, which always upset Father so, as it went against God, or so he would say. Anyway, we were looking at the snow. Emilie had returned from college that weekend, but she was not looking at the snow – she was in the rocking chair, reading a green- and gold-covered book, from time to time jotting down some notes in a small notebook that she always had with her, along with an unusual violet-coloured pencil. Never any other colour; always that strange violet. She was jotting things down, and we were doing nothing because outside it was snowing like never before. For some days now it had been snowing like this, and neither coachmen nor intrepid riders ventured onto the highway. Father was at my side, yet I could sense that from time to time he would surreptitiously glance at Emilie in the rocking chair. He was frowning because he was thinking. He was never relaxed, Father. He declared that it would stop snowing any moment now, because it never snowed for more than three consecutive days.

"It simply isn't natural," he announced, and then remained silent. But then I saw him observing Emilie, and I knew that he wasn't thinking about the snow.

At length he returned to the topic of the climate, although initially it seemed as if this subject was stuck in his throat while his mind was elsewhere. Father had been one of the principal characters involved in the construction of the Northampton Lunatic Asylum. I cannot avoid it: each time I see those red walls, those exterior walls covered in foul-smelling, dreadful ivy, those deranged faces at those accursed windows, I cannot help but think that Father could have imagined such a place exclusively for Emilie.

The day that the poet John Clare died, interned in the asylum for twenty-three years, Emilie cried as if she had caught a glimpse of her own destiny: seeing him captive within those towers that oozed madness day after day, keeping alive through writing poems about birds that build nests, poems of nests with wings, feathers of ivy, stalks and ropes, day after day, while outside, in the world, his children ended up dying before him. That place held a dreadful attraction for Emilie. Whenever we would go to Northampton for any reason – shopping, social visits, some event – she would insist in going to, or at least passing by the asylum. Soon after the asylum had been built, with Father at the head of the committee, it became one of the most recommended of such places in the whole of America, and its renown for excellent scientific research even reached Europe. However, as its fame increased so did the number of chronic patients admitted on a daily basis: dispossessed, abandoned, cast out from society, demented, poets, artists, opium and laudanum addicts from the cities, defiant alcoholics and prostitutes, the melancholics, dragged under by loss or injustice. They were all fated to take up their residence within the lunatic asylum, sealed off from the world behind the metal bars in one or other of the recently added new wings – buildings that seemed to be added on one side and amputated on the other. The asylum was a vast monster of madness and neglect, from which nobody ever left.

The soul, Emilie would say, chooses its own company, and closes the door behind itself.

That asylum should be closed down for good. Its loathsome ivy should be left to smother the walls right up to the roof, and to gnaw away at the windows starting with the bars and pushing into the interior of those wings and their miseries. They should have closed down that place while Emilie was still alive. Perhaps some of the magnetic attraction of madness cut with decay would have modified things a little.

5

For Every Bird, a Nest (Sue)

To see such a bird in such a nest...
– Lord Byron

*J*ust as the suffering and rebellious determination of Jane Eyre fascinated her, so was Emilie enamoured with Sue, so much closer and more real than the English landscape of the Brontës. In some respect, Sue represented the ambition that Emily had harboured for herself. One day, I remember, a good while before her death, Emilie saw the photograph of Mattie dressed in a new outfit with a splendid hat for her graduation, and she said: "that is how I would have liked to have been: that same defiant expression, that same confidence... such a beautiful and adorable girl!" Emily and Austin adored Sue and they defended her in a way that was as unconditional as it was fierce.

Susan Gilbert was the youngest of seven siblings. Her family were from Greenfield although early on her father brought them to Amherst. Mr Gilbert was a tavern-keeper, a man of little luck, perhaps too generous, perhaps too idealistic, or perhaps simply too weak to maintain alone a family of nine. The kindest neighbours used to take them food, and blankets for the children, seeing that Mr Gilbert could rarely satisfy the basic needs of his brood. Sue always remembers having survived her impoverished childhood thanks to the charity of others, and yet she also remembers her childhood with more disdain than pity. When they moved to Amherst, old Gilbert took the management of the tavern and stables on Main Street, the only proper level street of the town. But even so he could not make ends meet, and the neighbours continued helping them out.

Sue was scarcely five years old when her mother finally succumbed to the pain, the impotence and the misery of her overburdened life. All of Sue's brothers and sisters, aside from those who had already died of badly treated illness, ended up at the mercy of an insolvent, soon to be also a drunk, father. Four of the children at this time went to live in Geneva, New York, in the care of their maternal aunt. Soon after this Gilbert himself died in Amherst, bequeathing only debts and a name registered in the list of bankrupts.

Perhaps it is because of the poor example set by her father that Sue's capacity to tolerate economic uncertainties has always been very limited. Following her marriage to my brother Austin, Sue Huntington Gilbert transformed herself into Susan Dickinson, and in this way the surname Gilbert disappeared for ever from her life.

From the day that she left for Geneva, Sue wanted nothing more to do with her father, neither before nor after his death, or at least until many years after his death – to be precise, 1876 – when, owing to guilt or perhaps remorse, she called her youngest son Thomas Gilbert, the name of his grandfather. Father, our father, by this time was also dead, yet he had always been the substitute for the ideal father figure, serious and successful, that Sue so needed. She sought him out as an ally, and Father protected her like a daughter; and when she married Austin, Father did absolutely everything that she implicitly or explicitly asked for, so as to keep the new couple in the town. The construction of the Evergreens, only a few yards from our house, was one of the most treasured dreams for Sue, and was probably a contributing factor in their haste to wed, and their acceptance to remain in Amherst.

And yet, not one of us, ever, could stand up to that visceral, cruel and spiteful side of Sue. Well, perhaps Austin could, but that was only because this spitefulness would fall off his back like rain slipping off magnolia petals, leaving nothing but a gentle moistness. They both had strong temperaments, they were both excessive, fairly cruel and independent, they both loved money and the good things that money could buy. But it was Sue who could, and still can despite her age, hate with an inexhaustible intensity, just as she could love blindly and passionately despite obvious defects and faults. But above all she could hate.

At eighteen Sue returned from Geneva, New York, with the intention of settling in Amherst. In those days, if indeed she was not beautiful in the classical sense – that's to say pale and shapely – I would say that to see her was to inspire a certain envy, a terrible desire to be like her. Generally, Sue's mere presence in any place was enough to set off immediate whisperings and murmurings, as contrary to that fashion of languid step and pale illness, Sue had a dark complexion, dark slanted eyes, hair as dark as those eyes, always held up in an unkempt fashion with a ribbon, and in her bearing not an ounce of lethargy, quite the opposite. I would even say that at times there was something not feminine about her, something simply vital and magnetic. She was beautiful like a wild deer is beautiful, or a crow soaring. She was quick to laugh, quick to make cutting remarks, and utterly incapable of apologizing. She knew almost as much as Emily, having spent longer than most enlightening herself as a true autodidact; but her mind was sharper and more analytical than my sister's. Had she been born a man, I am certain that she would have excelled in business – she had the ability without ever being able to use it. She, as much as Emilie, resented having been born a woman. In one of the habitual notes that Sue sent in reply to one of Emilie's, she said: "If the nightingale can sing even with his breast pierced by the thorn, why cannot we, Emily?"

She had weathered eighteen years of poverty and resentment when she returned to the house of her sister Harriet, who was married to the town storekeeper, William Cutler. She was the one member of the family still living on charity, this time that of her brother-in-law, whom she detested. Because of his stiffness, his puritanical background, and because simply that was the way he was, Cutler never missed the opportunity to let both Sue and her sister Martha know that he was providing for them, and that they were both a burden of commiseration that only family ties and the love for his wife allowed him to bear with patience. Sue hated with all her being that which she and Emilie called "the puritan recipe", whose most perfect and recently baked product was William Cutler. Just like Emilie, although for different reasons, she felt that pressing need to stand out, and yet unlike Emilie, in a way that made her the centre of the cultural life of the town, overcoming humiliation and the privations of her childhood – impressing people. She was anxious that her financial situation, miserable for so many years, would finally ennoble her: she could not tolerate the idea of dependence, of not having money, of asking for loans. Yes, of this I am certain. But I am also certain that her prodigious intelligence was not a product of necessity, but more the opposite, it was *thanks* to this quality of intelligence that she could get to where she is still today, even to rising, thanks to God, above the name of my brother.

Emilie always said that "Susie knew no fear", and she was right about that, although I, over the years, have begun to believe that *we* were the ones who never fully fathomed the extreme depths of her fears. Emilie herself has said this in one of her poems that Sue still has in her possession:

> To pity those who know her not
> Is helped by the regret
> That those who know her know her less
> The nearer her they get.

Splendid poem! As much Emilie's as Susan's at the same time.

The enigma of Sue was, for my sister, the most powerful of her attractions. She never stopped loving her, venerating her, even when rumours now suggest that they stopped seeing each other, that owing to Austin's adulterous affair Sue felt betrayed by Emilie, by me, by all the Dickinsons.

Sue's friendship with Emilie and with Austin began around the year 1850. That year was particularly difficult for my sister, seeing that all of us, including Sue, had decided to convert to the faith of Christ. All of us aside from Emilie. To find Christ, to recover inner peace through the glory of purification, the forgiveness of our sins and through endless prayer was our exclusive objective. Those who publicly acknowledged having found Jesus were admitted into the New Church. Those who doubted, or those who were not prepared to declare it publicly, were segregated. Father was transformed, Austin did so reluctantly, and I was the most convinced. But I must say in my defence that it was something of a fashion at the time to declare that one had been possessed by the "heavenly light", by a "supernatural benevolence" that invaded our everyday acts, by an "inexplicable and powerful faith" that made us love our neighbour and live according to the purest feelings. My poor sister could not understand what on earth this was all about. Sometimes she would call me aside, stare at me in the eyes trying to discover what it was that I felt as a divine possession, where this power lay that we all declared to have found, that anomalous and contagious figure of Christ. Many other times she would study my entranced expression, my movements, which before had been brusque and precise and which had now been transformed into gestures of praise, like those of a weightless spirit, and she would search in these peculiar transformations for the root of this performance, the unnameable source of this farce. She knew that I was capable of it, just as I was capable of mimicking any member of the townsfolk. But she found nothing conclusive, and she would retire agitated until the next examination, so great were my confidence and my ability to convince myself with the whole affair.

Father, fortunately, was by no means rigid when it came to matters of faith. Even today I doubt whether he himself was converted through honest, inner desire, or whether he felt that his work for the community in some respect demanded it. They say in the town, as a joke, that the vicar urged Father to seek Christ in his capacity as a lawyer, seeing as for him to do so as a human being and believer was not possible. The sad thing is that it was not simply a pleasantry, but the honest truth. For example, he reproached Emilie for nothing, but she, while still at Mount Holyoke, felt obliged by the authorities to spend hours by herself in the chapel, under instruction to pray without restraint to find Christ, always with pointless and amusing outcomes. "Vinnie, the light of Christ is somewhat opaque, yellowish, is it not?" she would ask after her ordeal. "Vin, does one feel in one's heart? But how? Does the heart stop, or beat more quickly?" "Oh Miss Fowler, I believe I may have dozed off while praying, but I must assure you that even in my dreams I didn't manage to see Christ..."

My poor sister, and there were we so mesmerized, so captivated by the divine light and the power of conversion! That was the only thing that Sue could not come to terms with in Emily: everything else – novels, poems, ideas, philosophy – all that Sue said or thought, she would share with Emily, as if by magic. But all this about the light of Christ she was unable to share.

In 1851 Sue left for Baltimore to take up the post of schoolmistress. She left without having made too many plans, almost without telling anyone, one of her many futile attempts to escape the house of Cutler, to find some means of supporting herself other than the expected route of marriage, religious seclusion or the streets of Washington or Philadelphia. She lived miserably throughout that year, hating the job, homesick for a home that never even existed. She earned less than two hundred dollars in total, scarcely having enough to return and not have to ask for money for a couple of months. But she went in any case, alone, and that was the attitude that Emilie most venerated, and yet the attitude that most destroyed her. Sue never asked Emilie anything, like that time that she went to New York to hear Jenny Lind, when she knew full well that Lind would give concerts in Northampton, only a few miles from Amherst, and that we would surely go and see her. Sue always moved according to her own will. On that occasion she asked her brother for money, and when she received no response, she accepted the invitation from a friend in Geneva, and set off without a chaperone, without a sister, without anyone, alone. Her fame as an independent spirit, even as a libertine, grew in the town because of these outlandish escapades, but all this only increased admiration from Emilie and Austin, and envy from those who, like myself, felt ourselves insufferably parochial and *demodées* alongside her.

Finally, following lengthy meanderings and negotiations with Father concerning the place where they would live, Sue said yes to Austin. We all thought that Emilie would die with the happiness of having Sue so close; the letters and notes between them flew from house to house on a daily basis, and continued like that for years. Thanks to her strength of character, Sue managed to forge a home, the Evergreens, and a family with Austin, so close to our house, but without accepting nor imposing any conditions upon this new coexistence. So much so, that at times we were merely neighbours whose yards backed on to each other.

6

Home Is Something Sacred

*T*o speak about Emilie, about Sue and about our youth, to speak about our life in general, can only really make sense within the slow context of this town.

A definition of God, as my sister once said. To define home is to define God.

And, if truth be known, there was nothing more terrible than God on a cold winter's night; the bells of the church tolling amidst the darkness and that cold, blue, deathly light of the cemetery, the streets, and the yards covered by an almost phosphorescent snow, the houses of the town all in semi-darkness like small defenceless animals, the black, dry trees, and the long cold silence. Yes, the silence of a night of storm and snow in Amherst was – and still is, only less so – the terror of God, the melancholy of God, something unsustainable, something barely tolerable so close to the warm glow of home. We could feel the wind from behind the protection of the library windows as one might hear someone who has lost his reason cry out in the darkness, with the same sorrow and helplessness. For many days we might not leave the house, only the menfolk would go out to try to shovel away some of the snow from the entrance. During those days the basement and the pantry would become the most frequented places of the house, for fetching the wood that had been stacked there during the clear afternoons. The glow from the fires and the flickering light of the candles was all we had during that early falling darkness. One's eyes would tire quickly, the habitual and undemanding tasks would become exhausting and one's whole being would go numb from such a lengthy captivity. There was nothing to do, and each of us went about our own occupations as best as we could: Father would read his solemn books, Mother would darn or sew, Emilie would write or would likewise read, always in her rocking chair with her book held up close to her eyes, Austin would seek excuses to storm off in a bad mood and lock himself in his room, and I would spend my time simply watching them from a chair, with my pussy cats on my lap.

Spring would always arrive, however, and the sugar harvest and the flowers once more, and the valley would renew itself in the long days of summer, and by that time all of us in the town would have forgotten the drudgery of winter. People would be out in the streets, or would tarry awhile at the door of one of the few stores and chat about the events of the day and the news in the *Springfield Republican*, the coach to Northampton would run four times a day until nightfall, there and back, and the feuds between the two towns started again, as in every season, and only because the snow no longer reduced them to identical spots at either frozen bank of the Connecticut.

Northampton, for example, had a bank and a courthouse and, as a result, any matter of commercial or legal nature would inevitably have to be resolved there. The women would make the most of the long hearings that their husbands or fathers were attending to charge down to Lathrops to look at the newly acquired fabrics and other items brought in directly from Washington or Boston or even, in some cases, from Paris. The lady who bought herself a Parisian hat or an embroidered shawl or some pointed shoes for dancing – dancing shoes when we were unable even to organize a quadrille worthy of the graduation! – *that* lady would be the topic of discussion throughout Northampton and even, what's more, in Amherst, always envious of sophistication. There was a theatre in Northampton which always figured in my dreams as the theatre where I would appear on the arm of Salvini: the scarlet and gold curtains, the boxes for the gentry, and the great stage where the very same renowned figures who appeared in Boston or Philadelphia would appear. Gatherings in Northampton were relaxed, permissive, almost criminal to the eyes of the parish of Amherst. Men and women would play cards together at the games tables where they also served alcohol, and the men could smoke and converse freely without being attacked through insinuation at the weekend mass. Our Amherst only had to its credit a respected college, but everything in the life of that community was governed by religious and moral rules. Not in vain did Mark Twain so publicly make such fun of such places, saying that the bored faces of those towns should be imprinted onto the coins, so characteristic are they.

As for anything else, the only event was graduation. Let's call it the one social happening of the year, although the flirting and dancing were reduced to a minimum that the adults, as much as the young folk, deemed acceptable. The old Sewing Society to a certain degree made up for all that was prohibited in the "academic" circles. Here the young "ladies" and young "gentlemen" would get together in the parlour of some or other house, where we young ladies would sew clothes for charity, and the gentlemen would talk about horses and journeys. Two chaperones would set up huge silver trays and would serve tea and those cakes and cookies that we girls would have slaved over preparing a long while prior to the event. The social code dictated that these gatherings were essentially informal, and so if I talk ironically about young ladies and gentlemen it is only because at those gatherings I have heard the most dreadful blasphemies and the vilest swear words coming from the shy mouths of the girls, and I have taken part with the other girls in the most blatant, almost scandalous acts of flirtation in the dark stairway, away from the watchful gaze of the chaperones.

It now all seems absurd to me, and I cannot but suffer it again as a vague, embarrassing memory. I remember Emilie, and indeed Sue, making the most of the Society gatherings to initiate debates and weighty arguments with a select few sensitive young men of fortunate intellect, amongst whom one could always justly count my brother Austin. The remainder of us, aside from talking, sewing and flirting, would dedicate ourselves to concocting the gossip and the stories that would make up the poor diet of unimaginative material for that week.

Time passed, and Amherst could not even boast about its college: the widow of Smith Sr., one of the richest characters of the state, founded a college exclusively for women in the centre of Northampton.

And yet there was an episode that stirred up the region to perhaps the same level as the events of 1871, soon after the visit of Colonel Higginson, that I'll try to explain. In the collective memory the incident in question is remembered by the name of "the episode of Miss Lester".

Carrie Lester, who at that time was still under twenty years of age, was without doubt one of the most beautiful girls of Amherst. Nobody doubted that she would marry

well, and her mother had in mind either a cleric, a teacher,
or a man of law. However, it so happened that a Russian
count, named Mitkiewicz – Eugene Mitkiewicz, if my
memory serves – arrived in Amherst at the invitation
of one of the influential families. He was not the most
handsome of all men but he was cultured, his manners
were impeccable, if a little too delicate, and he had a perfect
pronunciation of both French and German that evinced
sighs from all the young girls of marrying age, and not only
them. With time, as was to be expected, young Miss Lester
and the Count fell in love, and everyone, aside from her
close family, were fully aware of the romance, and indeed
to a certain degree protected the lovers. The situation
could sustain itself thanks to the Count's business in New
York, and during the week he had to spend more time
there than in Amherst. Finally, when on one occasion he
telegraphed young Miss Lester to tell her that he would
be arriving the following day, her mother intercepted the
letter and deduced immediately what was coming to pass
with her daughter. Obviously the telegraph never reached
its destination, but not only that: her stepfather, Professor
Tyler, sought assistance in preventing the Count from
reaching the town, either that or compelling him because
of his actions to leave town, threatening him with setting
two hundred students upon him if he attempted in any
manner to approach his stepdaughter. The Count, even
with his distinguished and peaceful manners, was not
one to allow others to intimidate him, casting aside the
threat as a rather humourless joke. And so he proceeded
to his destination at the hotel. From there he sent a second
note to his loved one, which his loved one did not receive;
a third, which she didn't receive either; until at length,
exasperated, but thwarted in his plans to reach the house
in person, he offered one hundred dollars to whomsoever

might be capable of delivering, within two hours, a fourth note to Miss Lester, in which he urged her to meet him at the hotel whence they would flee to New York. The Irish woman who worked for the family managed to contact Miss Lester in an improvised manner, as the girl, locked in a room upstairs in the house, had managed to escape through the window. And so while the one was leaving the house, the other was heading towards it, and the two of them almost collided. No sooner had she read the note, than the young girl took to her heels to seek the safety of the Count's arms, and by the time Professor Tyler arrived at the hotel, the two lovers had already spent more than two hours together in the bedroom. They say that Tyler barged in without knocking, and that the happy faces of the couple served only as a futile gesture of explanation. Nevertheless, for Professor Tyler the damage to his honour had been inflicted; and that being the case he commanded Miss Lester to leave the Count that instant and to return home. But she, embracing the noble Russian, replied, "only dead would I leave him," and no amount of exhortation would move her.

That Sunday the Count went to the church with his betrothed, and I can promise that not one member of the congregation paid the slightest attention to the sermon: that morning all eyes were riveted upon the couple, who both stared at the pulpit with that happy innocence that only those who have been in love can understand. The next day, against the wishes of her mother, they took the train to New York to celebrate the wedding there. However the wedding was delayed even longer. Enamoured as he was, and yet anxious to keep the family of his future bride happy, the Count promised to spend a year abroad and to return to her with this "proof of his love". Clearly this "proof" constituted something less ethereal than mere love, which the poor fellow had quite clearly proved in extreme. Exactly one year after his departure, the Count returned to America armed formidably with this famous "proof of his love", and by this stage nobody could raise any further objections – aside from her mother, who excused herself from the wedding claiming a severe attack of nerves.

Count and the new Countess Mitkiewicz never returned to Amherst, and although the title of nobility was extended to the bride – a title that her mother wasted no time in defending as if it were her own – I doubt whether this title can claim any more valour than the courage of the two lovers themselves.

In all other respects, as we all know, the true measure of the scandal, the real issue at the heart of the matter, that was for the first time the envy of Northampton, were those two hours that the lovers spent in the hotel bedroom – that well-known secret – from the moment she ran to the arms of the Count to the moment Professor Tyler, by now too late, burst into the bedroom.

7

The Hour of Lead

This is the Hour of Lead
Remembered, if outlived,
As freezing persons recollect the Snow –
First – Chill – then Stupor – then the letting go –
– E. Dickinson (1862)

I'm ceded – I've stopped being theirs –
The name they dropped upon my face
With water, in the country church
Is finished using now,
And they can put it with my dolls,
My childhood, and the string of spools,
I've finished threading – too –
– E. Dickinson (1862)

I must have been over thirty when I discovered how our lives were going to be from then on. Not just my life but also Emilie's. It was soon after I saw Joseph Lyman for the final time, that afternoon in which he suddenly appeared like a ghost in Amherst, like the living dead, with his carriage laden with things for New York.

I felt nothing in particular following his visit. I mean, nothing beyond that sadness that resembles resignation. As I said earlier, he could just as well simply exist in my memories, and that if I do remember him now with that clarity that flatly contradicts my pretence at indifference, it is not because I still think about him. Good grief, what more could I want now than still to love a man with that insane passion of youth, even for just a moment? No, I say again, that is not the reason. I remember him because that moment marks the sudden change in Emilie's extravagant behaviour with regard to occasional visitors to the house. Emilie's reluctance to deal with real living people, that I have already mentioned on other occasions, the shadow of her dress upon the stairs, her ridiculous excuses for leaving the room that over time neither she nor I would need to use, the trays with wine and poems, fruits and cookies. All these things.

I, who acted as the go-between for Emilie with the world behind closed doors, transformed myself rapidly for Father and Mother into the go-between with the world *outside*. At that time the marriage of Austin and Sue was a star that lit up the drab skies of Amherst, with Ned crawling along the corridors and Mattie soon to be born, with the parties and gatherings that invariably featured characters like Emerson or Reverend Whilston, literary figures, musicians, painters, the Northampton society, basically. Austin, little by little, began to take over from Father the duties of the business, taking charge of the decisions of the College, which allowed Father the time to dedicate himself to the problems of the railroad or the Republican Party, or to the feeding of the birds in the garden. Mother was rejuvenated following the birth of Ned, bursting with a new energy, a more expansive mode of interaction with those around her, something in her look that we had rarely detected before, or at least not very often – calmness. Pure and simple calmness. Even that mechanical gesture of being taken by the arm when going for a walk had changed. It was now she who would take Father's arm, she who would propose a stroll through the College gardens, she who would forget her cape and parasol, and it was we who, curiously enough, would run off to fetch these things for her.

Our niece and nephews were a tremendous source of joy and pride for Emilie and me, and even a source of competition for their fondness between us that included light-hearted conspiracies and amusing little traps. Our Ned and our Mattie, and later on our little Gilbert, but this time about which I speak little Gil had still not been born. Emilie and Sue would send each other notes on a daily basis through any of the boys or through me, notes with little poems, recipes, society gossip, letters from others that they would both read, newspaper cuttings or pages torn from books and underlined by both of them, each with a different colour. These small bundles of words in their most varied form flew between our house and the Evergreens, while Austin, amused, would indirectly participate in such a "frenzy of opinions", as he generally called it, and I would dedicate myself to transporting them from here to there and to discreetly bribing the children with pieces of marzipan bought in the local store.

Then, one morning, I discovered just that: that life would be like that day for ever. Just as it had been the day before so would it be the following day, and so would it be from then onwards. I discovered, not unhappily, that there was an order, a routine, to the things of each day, a measured rhythm that reflected life itself, in the same way that the cogs and wheels of a watch always work in the same way and are intrinsic to the passing of time. I understood that existence, or at least our existence, was like the body of a child whose bones have stopped growing. Henceforth, upon this cast of bones that had set without our knowing it, the only surprises would be granted by death, because even illness came within the sights of predictability.

Far from feeling frustrated by such a perspective, Emilie not only accepted her unyielding cast, her definitive shape, but she actually increased the density and consistency of it, making sure that by the time Judge Lord would appear in her life, this cast would be rigid as a suit of armour. The Queen had become trapped in her own wax mould, protected from interruptions, protected from the temptation of escape.

For me things were not so different. I had given up the possibility not so much of not having a family, but of having a man at my side, someone who would look after me, protect me, like Father had with us. I suppose that having lost true love once, I never wanted to replace it with a lukewarm approximation that would only serve to make me remember it for ever.

What *is* certain is that I had lost no ground in terms of my social life, quite the contrary, my circle of friends was small yet intense. Little by little I took the reins of the house, both the important decisions and, ever more, the day-to-day trivialities, to the point that when Father passed away, it was I who assumed the position as financial head of our modest domestic empire. Some time later Mother suffered a terrible fall down the stairs, and that selfless acceptance of my key role became a pressing need. With Mother in bed upstairs, intermittently subject to the most astonishing array of disabilities, I could no longer count on her. I could count on Emilie, that's for sure, but the truth is that she counted on me far more than I on her. And in any respect, by that stage, my role as the principal cog in the machine had become the most important and almost exclusive objective of my life.

Marriage was no longer an option for either Emilie or me. Had it ever been? We had both embraced solitude, but solitude was never a burden for a Dickinson, quite the opposite, it was more of a right, almost a privilege. One might even imagine that Emilie was the most privileged of the three of us, seeing that she plainly exercised her right to solitude – a right that, paradoxically, required my presence.

With the passing of the years we would gain a niece and two nephews, like three foster children, like three angels to guard and protect and to break the spell of our solitude. And we would have the whole of Austin's family just around the corner, our friends, letters, a house that contained us, a garden full of trees and flowers, a selection of cats, a dog and a library. All in all we had everything that gives texture to a life without a family to take charge of. A family that, I suppose, we would have expected as a right.

"Hope is the thing with feathers, that perches in the soul, and sings the tune without the words, and never stops at all."

My sister wrote that – in May 1861 if I believe in the date marked on the reverse side of the page. Emilie would often add random dates to her poems, dates that held no obvious connection to anything. We were still young then, we still had not seen Joseph for the final time, nor had I yet convinced myself that his marriage to Laura Baker was permanent, nor that I, his silly childhood sweetheart, had been left entombed for ever in the shadows of New England, amongst pure and innocent memories of the pre-war years. I would love to believe that in that year, 1861, we would still hold out, if a little foolishly, to that sweet bird of hope, singing our song ever more remote...

No, marriage had never been a valid option for either of us. And that is why I speak of the moment in which that doubt, that uncertainty that still left a chink through which a glimmer of hope could be seen, died within us. I'm referring to the moment that we both finally lost even the notion of the tremulous small bird singing in our breast. The only poem of mine that I retain dates from that other, special time. A scrap of paper that has proved far harder to get rid of than Joseph's letters, letters that I ended up burning one day in a rapture of hate. In no way whatsoever have I tried to convince myself that I am a poet, let nobody think that I could be capable of such arrogance. I have been unable to throw this poem into the fire, along with others of my most precious papers, because each time I read it, it reminds me of the profound transformation in my behaviour, not just Emilie's. And it reminds me of that moment in which this daily, almost affable, coexistence with pain began – pain and I existing at the limits of what is tolerable like two good neighbours resigned to sharing their backyard or their fruit garden.

I could have abandoned it
at the beginning
but no:
I let it survive.

I forced it to grow up
close to me
(I thought that by keeping it
I could teach it,
me, just me,
who hadn't learnt
anything yet).

To drink I gave it those things
that were disappearing from
the universe,
I fed it on ghosts,
that way, I thought,
its supply would never be exhausted.

I grew along with it:
to warm it
I glued on feathers,
clear feathers
like tears
that scarcely brushed it
and turned black;
I opened its orphaned eyes,
I held open the cloth of its eyelids
and forced it to see, always;

I put curved talons
on its still innocent feet
and borrowed wings on its back.

I placed him behind the doors of my
breast,
in a red hollow
(it pierces my lungs and breathes,
it cleaves to my heart to get warm.
I sustain it).

There it lived
until it was ready.

I opened the doors
and it went out.

It fluttered
half-heartedly
around the room
but soon it was back,
perched on my breast,
its slow black wings
in a raven's embrace.

It had learnt to open
by itself
the doors of its cage.

I wanted to train this sorrow
so it would leave me.
All I had managed
was to tame it.

Part Two

Of course – I prayed –
And did God care?
He cared as much as on the Air
A Bird – had stamped her foot –
And cried "Give me" –
My Reason – Life –
I had not had – but for Yourself –
'Twere better Charity
To leave me in the Atom's Tomb –
Merry, and Nought, and gay, and numb –
Than this smart Misery.

– E. Dickinson

8

Amuasbteiln (Austin & Mabel)

I

*A*muasbteiln could well be the name of some magic creature, secretly dwelling in the forests of New England and in the tales for children. Or perhaps he could be some goblin from Shakespeare to be blamed for inexplicable spells and enchantments. Or perhaps the hero of some archaic legend of barbarous Vikings. Or the name of an imaginary kingdom that we ourselves created as children to protect us, to protect our very childhood from growth and deterioration, like the Gondal of the Brontës. It could be all these things, to be sure, but it ended up being scarcely more than an unpleasant joke, a silly childish invention of my brother in order to register in the most sinister and disrespectful way his most dreadful betrayal.

Because my brother, William Austin Dickinson, "our beloved Austin", was a shameless adulterer throughout the last twelve years of his life.

Curiously, within the atmosphere of this poor town obsessed with appearances and with being "under the Lord's eternal vigilance", my brother has been venerated almost more than Father, which takes things to an even greater level of grotesque stupidity. Everyone knew about his deceit, everyone. Austin kept things out in the open, hiding only behind the transparency of and obviousness of his sin. Even so, or perhaps because of this, men respected him and the wives of these men esteemed and praised him publicly. Whether they did so privately or not I cannot say, just like I'll never know how people came to act so hypocritically. Maybe it's because freedom is a man's right that no man would ever conceive of sacrificing. Women, on the other hand, do not have the right but the obligation to tend to the sick and the dead. There's no avoiding this burden.

Amuasbteiln. A word that is really both their names, Austin and Mabel, each letter alternating. And it was this word that I found written on a piece of paper, along with a date: 13th December 1883. I assume, along with everyone else, that this is the date in which they consummated their relationship. Austin carried this paper in his wallet until the day he died, or, I should say, until the day that Sue found it while dressing him for his tomb. Even today she keeps it, and that scrap of paper is her vow of anger and bitterness. I also imagine that Mabel would keep amongst her treasures an identical paper, with the identical word, along with an identical date.

Mabel Loomis Todd, for that is her full married name, was born the same year as the wedding of Austin and Sue. Her father, indeed, was the same age as Austin, and in every respect Mabel could have been my brother's daughter, like an elder sister to Mattie. I can certainly remember the occasions that Mabel would spend the night at the Evergreens with Mattie, after the piano lessons, after dinner, when it was by now too late or the snow was coming down too hard to have the carriage made ready to take her to the hotel, or, later, to Dell, crossing the small hill that separates the Evergreens from the Todd's house.

Was there any justification, any mitigating factor for this clandestine love between Austin and Mabel? After so many years and in the light of all that has happened and all that Mabel tried to do after my brother's death – I think there is not. There is now nothing left in me that could be swayed to the contrary, no part of me that would believe any justification now. For Austin was lover and benefactor for her and her husband at the same time. The land whereon they built Dell, the house they've lived in since they moved to Amherst – Austin gave it to them for nothing. Austin fought for no reward for her husband's contract at Amherst College. And finally, that fame that Mabel built for herself as a lecturer and as a woman of letters – Emily Dickinson, firstly, and then I, secondly, gave this to her. For nothing.

At night, when these tired old eyes of mine can scarcely stand the light of the logs burning in the grate, I try in vain to look for the root of so much evil, that exact point at which destiny took a wrong turn, at which Providence abandoned us to the luck of the Devil.

When did it all begin? Why? Various episodes appear in my memory, all of them clearly a prelude to the storm that descended upon our family, all associated with one particular year: 1882.

II

That was the year that Emilie and I were finally left alone, owners of that sacred place that had been the Dickinson family house, and which henceforth would be our own, personal, kingdom.

We were by now well-accustomed to life without Father, and soon to life without Mother, bedridden for so many years upstairs, at the mercy of what is probably the cruellest blow a person can suffer: an inert body but with all the senses intact.

Our family would then be limited to a routine of friendly interaction with the house of Austin and Sue, with traffic flowing between us, particularly from me to them, and from Ned, Mattie and little Gilbert to us, always keen to try Aunt Emilie's new cookies or to describe in detail the nasty accidents in the morning paper with Aunt Vinnie. I remember Gil, for example, tirelessly chasing my pussy cats one afternoon, the poor terrified animals trying to escape, all under the approving gaze of my sister. I remember Mattie, as an adolescent, the day she brought to the house yard after yard of muslin to make herself a dress, so much material that we could have wrapped the entire house in. And I remember Ned, the afternoon in which he charged into the kitchen covered from head to toe in snow, telling us about how one of Queen Victoria's subjects, an Englishman who had awarded himself the title of Professor of Aesthetics, had disembarked in New York dressed like a veritable clown in a burgundy velvet coat, an ermine fur around his neck, lace sleeves and lacquered riding boots, and that he had uttered the most preposterous and shameless declarations about his genius. English smugness knew no bounds, Ned continued, this character had all the pretentious intellectuals of New England in the pocket of his famously short breeches.[5] I remember Sue and Austin, still close and happy together,

---

5   In 1882 Oscar Wilde disembarked in New York, whence he began his only tour of North America, delivering his famous declaration, "I have nothing to declare except my genius." From that moment until the time that he finally returned to Europe after many months of his tour, he fed the local press with his declarations and the intellectual circles with his ideas. New England, however, too puritanical for Wilde's provocations, received him with a coldness which Wilde later described as "worse than the English, which is saying something".

enjoying long drives in the buggy, or setting off for Boston to buy some bizarre fashionable item for the Evergreens. I remember Emilie and Sue heatedly arguing over ridiculous modern issues, like the existence of consciousness after death, or the possibility that Man was the distant nephew of chimpanzees. And I remember myself, on my calm yet continuous activity around town, visiting the church to pray in silence, surrounded by the peace of a God who was ever more distant from the God that the Reverend spoke about.

And so, soon after this peaceful – at least that's how I remember it – year had begun, misfortune began, little by little, like a wrathful god, to untie the secure knots of our destinies.

Spring had scarcely arrived when news came from Philadelphia about the death, from sudden pneumonia, of the Reverend Charles Wadsworth. According to the newspaper, he spent the last days of his life prostrated in bed at the mercy of fierce, consuming delirium. Finally, in the early morning of the third day, he said aloud in a clear voice: "Please close the Bible now," and died that instant.

When I read the news to Emilie she said with a smile: "He was not delirious, Vin. He was preparing the path before him, and he spoke directly to God. He had no need of intermediaries. Besides, nobody addressing God could have a 'regular' conversation with Him, do you not think?"

I had just read to her of the death of one of her dearest friends, and Emilie, smiling, simply corrected what she took to be an error in the text of the newspaper.

"Did you know about it?" I asked.

In answer to my question Emilie showed me the date of the newspaper: it was more than ten days old. She had known for ten days. For ten days and she hadn't said a word, neither to me nor to Maggie. Why hadn't she spoken to me when she found out?

"Why, Vinnie? Why does the sun shine? I think perhaps nobody could answer that. Some things are just so, Vin."

Yes, some things are just so, and I had learnt a long time before to accept the "just so" of the things of my sister. Like when she would say, on those rare occasions that she accepted a visitor, "I wish for no witnesses," which invariably referred to that which she and Sue called "the North-East Passage". The passage in question was the dark corridor that led to the dining room and to the kitchen pantry, and to the secret stairway that rose to the first floor next to the bedrooms of Father and Mother, that nobody ever really used. Halfway up this flight of stairs, protected from the view of other people, Emilie would listen to the conversations of my guests, even her own guests. She would listen to the piano or she would circle down to the kitchen to prepare their souvenirs in small trays covered with linen cloths – flowers and a glass of wine or a slice of cake.

Sometimes, when night has fallen outside and I go to close the dining-room windows and check that the fire in the kitchen has been put out, I catch out of the corner of my eye the flash of her white dress on the stairs as she quickly flees before any sudden noise; fleeing like a hare, a sparrow or a squirrel. But when I approach I find the stairs empty and in shadow. Maggie says that Emilie's ghost lives in the North-East Passage, a ghost with long red hair who carries an oil lamp in her hand, going up and down the stairs, occasionally entering the pantry and rummaging in the sacks of corn or arranging all the spoons in a perfect line on the kitchen table. Maggie says that the ghost likes doing this, and to please her she often leaves the kitchen utensils in disarray upon the table, to find them the following morning once more aligned symmetrically as always.

Poor Maggie, perhaps I should let her know that this passion for symmetry has run in the Dickinson blood since the days our ancestors invaded England. Perhaps I should also confess to her that it is I, and not the supposed ghost, who arranges things in the kitchen when she is not there.

Only one thing prevents me from doing so – doubt. For there are days in which I cannot recall having arranged anything, and yet it turns out that in the morning the kitchen utensils are laid out in immaculate symmetry on the table. Because of this I, before anyone else, doubt the reliability of my own memory, and I fear that those gaps, those exceptional circumstances, follow a pattern that at this stage in my life I can even discern, which excludes my little performances to amuse poor Maggie. But if I do not yet forget my own actions, how can it be? It is then that I hear the calm and serious voice of Emilie deep within me saying:

"Why does the sun shine? Some things are just so, Vin."

III

But none of this has anything to do with poor Wadsworth. It has more to do with that particular manner of my sister for doing things, for saying or not saying things, and for suffering these same things in silence. The Reverend, as I said, had died in the springtime. Soon after this, with everything prepared for marrying Emilie and taking her to live with him in Salem, Judge Lord suffered another dreadful stroke that left him at death's door, from which he only partially recovered by the autumn.

Then, in the month of November, Mother died.

She had been for a good few years now laid up in bed upstairs, having fallen down the stairs and broken her hip. From that moment on she had languished in her room with a martyr's resignation, attended day and night by Emilie and me. Her body, which had never been particularly robust, wasted away day by day, inexorably, beneath the bedspreads that she would knit as her only pastime. I would arrange her dark hair into a large plait that I would do up in a bun, rather like one might play with a doll's hair; and I would arrange the ribbons of her silk shawl, the only item of clothing that, if we were correct in our assumption, was bought exclusively for the eyes of Father. Emilie would say that no sooner had she said "goodnight Mother" than she would find herself back in the room the following morning opening the shutters and ventilating the room and saying "good morning Mother", handing her a cup of tea with bread and jam for breakfast. So pressed were we by the daily effort of comforting her and relieving her daily suffering of immobility that we never noticed that her breathing was slowing down, until the moment in which it practically stopped altogether.

During the day I would head into town for the daily chores – "the matters of state" as Austin and Emilie called these duties – to the general store, the drugstore, the post office. Meanwhile Emilie would be looking after Mother, waiting for the sacred moment when "Vinnie has returned from the world", and then we would swap roles until nightfall so that Emilie could freely devote herself to her own things. "Vinnie has returned. God be praised!" she would whisper as she shut the door to Mother's room with a succinct, ironic, yet naturally generous comment about Mother's mood that day: "All afternoon Penelope has been demanding violet wool, *softened* violet wool or nothing."

"She wishes for no more pancakes for a few days, thank you very much." "Sheepskin works very well for relieving the bedsores, so much so that she has asked for some paper in order to thank Mrs Miller for the wine of last week, and why not a little glass to try now?"

Mother's mood rarely changed at dinner time, and as such Emilie's information was always useful to me to deal with these unusual needs of the infirm, and even to entertain her with some incident of one of the neighbouring towns – incidents that I would often invent according to how I gauged her mood and interest.

I must confess, however, that I could never put up with Mother's illness. I would spend hours by her side reading the newspaper to her, or telling her about the gossip going around town, but I could not bear to see her like that, gradually shrinking, growing daily more transparent. I couldn't bear the acrid smell of the medicines, her immobility, her slow and doleful gaze. That is why I would head outdoors upon any excuse: to the dressmaker for Emilie, to pay a bill here or there, to see the new flowers in so-and-so's garden. The greater the distance from home the better. That is also why I believe Mother clung to those moments with me and waited patiently for one of those moments in which to die. One night I went to tuck her in and cover her with the blankets and wish her goodnight, and as I was leaving the room I heard her voice, scarcely more than a whisper, like a little bird if a little bird could speak:

"Vinnie. Don't leave me."

When I returned to her side she had closed her eyes. I called for Emilie who was downstairs in the kitchen, shouting that Mother was dying and that she should come up immediately. While I heard the quick steps of my sister running up the stairs I held my mother's hand tightly in mine to give her strength, holding it against my breast to preserve that heartbeat a moment longer...

But when Emilie arrived at her side that hand that I held in mine was limp.

Later, Austin, Sue and the children arrived. Little Gilbert gazed at Mother's body with an expression of serene wonder in the face of death, a gaze that *I* would wish to have in front of death, in front of everything. It was neither fear, nor pain, nor compassion nor weakness. Just wonder.

"Vinnie. Don't leave me." Those were her final words and I remember that every time I think of how often I was not at her side when I should have been, like Emilie had been, still and faithful, despite everything.

Her death, and one of the harshest and most punishing winters that I can remember, left us alone in the house, defenceless beneath a roof that no longer protected a family, but two survivors.

IV

By then Mabel Loomis Todd had already arrived in Amherst with her husband, the dazzling professor of astronomy, David Todd.

She would later edit Emilie's poems and would become the lover of my brother Austin. She would break the heart of my nephew Ned, and the heart of Sue, although for different motives. She would claim for herself the glory, the fame and the land of my family, and aside from the land, she would keep it all.

She would spell the downfall of the Dickinsons.

And yet, Mabel was a type of angel.

Yes, I will admit it. I, who have come to dismiss her

so much, recognize that she was at the beginning an innocent and special person, even though before meeting
her, so much praise of her had inspired in me the deepest
mistrust. I should have followed my instinct instead of
believing blindly the embellished judgement of others.
When she arrived in Amherst she was still a very young
and elegant lady, with a slender waist and small shoulders,
fashionably dressed but always with her own personal
touches. She would often paint flowers on her dresses,
which I remember as a detail that I adored. She sang
beautifully, as I suppose she still does, and she played
the piano. She had lived in the big cities, and her primary
passion was talking. It was her means of seducing: to
talk and to lie. To lie in a refined way, withholding certain
details, telling only half-truths. I do not think, however, that
Mabel was particularly intelligent. Intelligence, if there is
any particular sign that defines it, if it can be identified in
others like a mark on the skin, is something that is found
in one's sense of humour and in one's melancholia; not
in anguish and passionate outbursts of sadness, but in the
melancholia of poets, a special capacity for introspection
tied to a certain internal calm, to that which is known as
inner life or spiritual wealth. To be able to be alone is a sign
of intelligence, to tolerate is a sign too, as it is to laugh.
Mabel was astute, and for that reason she could perhaps
mimic these attributes, but she lacked inner calmness, the
humility to laugh at anything that wasn't someone else's
mistake or embarrassment. That's what nobody knew, at
least at the beginning, and that's why she appeared to us
as an angelic being, perhaps a little highly strung, a little
dainty and exquisite, like a hummingbird.

Sue was immediately captivated by her, and, without the
slightest idea of what would happen later both to her

son Ned and her husband Austin, she opened her door
to her. Every day Mabel would take part in whichever
improvised party or gathering there might be taking place
at the Evergreens, she gave piano classes to Mattie, but
reserved her special charms for Ned, later transferring
them to Austin. Indeed it was Austin who initially begged
her to brighten the long afternoons of Mother's illness
at our house. She adored music, and from that evening
of Jenny Lind's concert both Emilie and I would attempt
to accompany her singing or at the piano, but neither
my sister nor I were ever particularly gifted, and scarcely
managed the most basic work of Mendelssohn, Beethoven
or Schumann, or simply those orthodox pieces used more
to exercise the fingers than for anyone's pleasure. Mabel
would read the score with an astonishing ease and speed,
so much so that I began to wonder whether she actually
was playing from memory and was making the gesture of
reading so as to impress us. Well, whether from memory
or not, the fact was she began to visit us from time to time
to cheer our evenings with her tales and her voice. From
upstairs, Emilie and Mother would always listen enraptured
to her, and Emilie would at times send down a couple of
verses written on a card in violet ink, or some flowers, or a
glass of wine as a sign of appreciation.

Towards the end of 1882, my nephew Ned, sweet Ned, fell
madly, blindly and openly in love with Mabel. Austin also
fell in love, but behind our backs, and Emilie and I, like
fools, insisted on denying it. Later, nothing would seem
dreadful enough for God to call a halt to the proceedings
there – no, nothing would induce Him to take pity on us.
Especially not on Emilie.

Suddenly, in the spring of 1883, everything appeared
to dissolve, to calm down as if all the hatred, anger and

pain of the previous months had never existed. An idyllic, treacherous calm invaded the collective spirit of the family, of Amherst, of the entire world. Ned, Mattie and Gilbert were still at the Evergreens, but nobody would have even imagined that little Gil would be leaving us soon – everyone was too worried about Ned.

By September, one of Ned's habitual attacks warned us that something was forthcoming. Illness was nothing new to Ned, on the contrary; he had been born with a particular condition that affected his nerves, something that throughout his infancy had seemed like a permanent languor, a distraction, that as a child had distanced him quite considerably from the other children. That secret melancholia in his eyes was thus more a product of the solitary games of a child who tires easily than of any illness as such. In time, however, especially with the approach of adolescence, he began to suffer fits. For years these attacks were infrequent and left no ill effects – in truth it was a blessing that Ned never remembered them – but, through misfortune, and with no possible cure, the attacks grew ever stronger. One morning in September, Mattie came to tell me about the attack of the previous night – always nocturnal – when the worst of the convulsions had finally subsided.

"It was after midnight," she related, "some lights were still burning and Mama and Papa were up watching that Neddie didn't swallow his tongue or crack his head on the floor. The fits are far stronger now, and Papa is better at helping Ned. But it's Mama who cannot bear to see him like that. She stands paralysed until Papa shouts at her that if she's not going to do anything then it's best she leaves the room and comes back later. Last night was like that. When I went down to the dining room to lock the door, I found Aunt Emily standing at one of the windows, but outside, amongst the rose bushes, as if wondering whether to come round to the back door. She was like a ghost. 'Aunt Emily,' I cried in my alarm. 'What are you doing standing out there so late?' 'Shhh,' she whispered, without moving from where she was. 'Is he better – oh tell me, is he better?' she asked.

"I told her that he was better, that the worst of it was now over, and I ran to the back door to open it for her, but by the time I'd opened it she'd gone. I could just make out Aunt Emily's nightshirt, black shawl, and loose hair as she quickly walked towards the Homestead."

Poor Mattie. What a dreadful fright she must have had.

Just as to be expected, as soon as Emilie returned from her secret trip to the Evergreens she came straight to my bedroom. She had in her hand a tray with a glass of wine and a slice of bread.

"Vin," she whispered, "are you awake?"

I, who not only had heard her leave but had moreover watched her from the sewing-room window, pretended that I was asleep, and that I would only wake reluctantly.

"Vinnie, I have to tell you something terribly important," she said, sitting on the edge of my bed with the tray on her lap.

"Emilie, what time is it?"

"One in the morning, Vinnie. Ned is better, there's no need to worry any further. For the moment, at least, the worst is over."

"And this is to celebrate that?" I asked, taking a sip of the wine.

"Hands off the tray you old glutton! This is for me. I need to calm my nerves."

Before leaving my room I asked her how she knew that Ned was better.

"I dreamt it," she replied.

Only at four in the morning did the lamp go out in her room.

$\mathcal{V}$

Ned's brother Gilbert had his eighth birthday on the first of August of that year. In our family there was no tradition of celebrating either birthdays or anniversaries, but that summer we did. It was part of that feeling of peace and spiritual blossoming that had taken hold of our souls, and that would last such a short time.

Towards the end of September Gil was confined to his bed with a fever that would not ease off for all our care and attention. The persistence of this fever, sapping the strength from his frail body too fiercely for one so young, alerted us to the presence of something far worse than merely influenza. On the first of that dreadful month of October the doctor diagnosed the illness. Gil had been playing with another boy, Kendall Emerson, in the mud of a shallow well, scarcely a week earlier, and where the other boy had caught no more than a common cold, along with a small cut on his finger, Gil, our Gil, had contracted typhoid; playing in exactly the same place, playing exactly the same game, in the same way, beneath the same sky, beneath the same God.

The infection was treacherous, deceptive, like everything that precedes the inevitability of death. The fever did not lose its grip entirely but Gil did appear to improve for a little while. Sue and Austin looked after him by night, and after a brief respite we all believed that the crisis had passed, that Gil's body had won the battle by itself.

We were wrong. That brief respite scarcely lasted a week. That very night the poor boy suffered a terrifying relapse, and both Emilie and I found ourselves running over to the Evergreens dressed just as we were in our nightshirts with a shawl over our shoulders. Emilie, I remember, was barefoot. A few days before she had twisted her ankle coming down the stairs, and because of this she limped and was unable to put a shoe on her swollen and bandaged foot. In the same way she charged around Sue's house barefoot with the help of a walking stick, flatly disregarding the doctor's advice and my orders.

"The only thing you can do, beyond praying, is to make the room as hygienic as possible," the doctor had said.

Sue and Emilie, by temperament as unlikely as each other to kneel down and pray, set about scrubbing and cleaning with bleach and then kerosene every last nook and cranny of Gil's bedroom. They then boiled the bedclothes and the curtains, along with some toys, for hours in the open air, and the books and everything that might harbour a germ was stripped from the bedroom. After two days of frenzy that left the floor bare and aseptic, they had to accept that the poor boy was breathing ever more slowly, and they had to abandon the disinfection and huddle close around little Gilbert's bed. For my part, I tried to keep Mattie and Ned company. The two poor little souls walked around as if they were lost, with expressions of pain and uselessness so terrible that my own heart bled with anguish before the impossible task of bringing them any comfort.

It was then that I perceived for the first time the change that had started to work through the soul of my brother. Poor Austin looked dumbfounded, blank. The gaze of a dead man.

Throughout those days of suffering we didn't allow ourselves to talk of anything other than Gil. Nobody asked after anyone other than the boy: had his fever gone down? Were the sheets wet with his sweat and needing to be changed again? Had they been able to give him his only medicine, which was water with a little salt? On the morning of the final day Emilie could no longer bear the vapours of disinfectant, the fatigue, the anxiety, and she finally succumbed and let herself slump silently against the wall in one of the corners of the room. Nausea and migraine had overcome her to such a degree that she had to be carried back to the Homestead, where, before we could put her to bed, she violently vomited. I helped her clean her face and dress and laid her in bed, helping her through a delirium that made her clench her fists to the point of wounding herself. I thought it was the fever, and that it would carry her off too. But no, it was little Gilbert's death, just after midnight, that closed the door on that chapter.

The morning following Gilbert's death was the darkest that I can or ever will remember. It was perhaps the beginning of that interminable agony that I mentioned earlier, closed off from God's mercy. Emilie was confined to bed, having regained consciousness but in a state of physical debility that prevented any activity. When she awoke she said that Gil, during the night while unconscious, had opened his eyes and had called out for the door to be opened, because outside *they* were waiting for him. Then the fever gripped him again and she could do no more than talk to him, hold his cold and wet little hands, and assure him again and again that they were waiting for him, angels as bright and beautiful as the sun, and that if God was merciful and allowed her, she too would go with him to keep him company on his final, unique and infinite journey.

"I could do nothing, Vinnie, nothing to hold him back," she ceaselessly repeated throughout that awful morning. "I couldn't clasp myself to him so that he would take me with him. I had to watch him die. I – I – who have nothing left in this world. Nothing."

During those days Emilie spoke thus about little Gilbert. She talked and talked about her pain with an unwholesome abandon, with an emphasis born in the shadow of delirium and nightmare. Human pain is selfish in its ignorance of everything that is not suffering, and perverse in its determination to stir its own miserable gruel without taking notice of anyone or anything. I myself could not even grant myself the luxury of crying for Gilbert, for my little rosy-cheeked, serious-looking darling, who would chase the pussy cats for hours only to come running to me to beg me to rescue them from the tree that they'd climbed in order to escape him.

Not I – I could not cry for him. I did hold his cold little body against my breast, when nobody was watching, and that was all. That and help Emilie in her grief while confiding to her that my own grief would gradually dry away, just like so many other things in my life had dried away.

Little Gilbert's death occurred at the beginning of October. One year later, as she was baking some of her blessed bread, Emilie suddenly lost consciousness and fell to the floor, fracturing her wrist and forearm. She remained on the kitchen floor unconscious for more than two hours, until Maggie returned from a shopping trip, found her, and dragged her up to her room. Doctor Bigellow was called at once, and yet, when Emilie saw me send for the doctor she began to protest, saying that it was merely a dizzy spell, that there was no need for a doctor for just that;

and she made such a fuss, which on any other occasion would have conquered anyone's will, but this time I was not going to allow her to take control. I sent for the doctor and also for Austin. With Austin in the house Emilie had to control her wrath, and dared not dismiss the good doctor Bigellow, who spent nearly an hour examining her. When the examination was over, he diagnosed that it could be the early stages of Bright's Disease, a slow and incurable illness of the blood that, as it advanced, would slowly consume her without causing her great physical suffering, only weakness and those fainting spells that could last up to a matter of hours. Or days. That is what Bigellow said when he left, that the end of my sister would be like the end of a candle that goes out of its own accord.

Emilie, for her part, never allowed another doctor to examine her. She never even allowed another doctor to enter her bedroom.

"All there is to see," she would say, "is perfectly visible from the door."

9

Funerals

She lay as if at play
Her life had leaped away
Intending to return –
But not so soon –
                – E. Dickinson

I

From the time of Doctor Bigellow's visit, I knew that Emilie's departure would occur far before mine. Some irreverent order, some order with no relation whatsoever to God had imposed its authority upon our family following the death of little Gilbert. It is true that Father and Mother had already left us, but until then death's cold order had been in balance, it had followed either its pattern or, I should say, its divine disposition, which ordains that everything that has completed its cycle of life – man, animal or plant – must die when it must die and cede its place to the ensuing birth of life. Balance, and at times also the will of God, is indispensable for that acceptance of fatality; and it was for that reason that we accepted first Father's departure and then Mother's, without question, without excessive suffering. And although grief is ever present, we had always known that one day they would not be among us, with the same certainty that one would know that winter is coming and that it is useless to rebel against such an act of nature.

But after the death of little Gilbert nothing would ever be natural again. Nothing.

One may imagine that what I'm saying is all mad ravings, that after all I am the youngest and the one who has survived, and as a result divine order remains intact. It is not like that: I am by far the least necessary, the least important of the three of us. Emilie was admired, perhaps envied, by many because of her extravagances, or even feared in secret. But despite that persistent chrysalis in which she lived, a greater light shone on her and only on her. Austin was Father's successor, a pillar of the community, the first to run to for advice, for money, or for political support. If Austin made known his opinion about some matter, whatever this matter may be, an opposing voice was unlikely to be heard, if indeed there was one at all. The whole of Amherst was on his side. They were capable of backing and supporting him, according to his wishes; averting their eyes when it was necessary, of course, against their customs and morals, as when he would pass with Mabel on his arm, lovingly holding her parasol like an enamoured schoolboy.

Austin and Emilie were each in their own way unknown to the people of Amherst, but the respect that was paid them, that reverence totally at odds with who they were, was basically the same. The rest of us led what one might call mediocre lives; or maybe I should say that mine was mediocre. Just like Mother, and to my shame, I've lived an ordinary life, aside from, perhaps, the detail of not having sought the false safety of marriage.

I feel that I have been left tied to this world without deserving it, only to try to preserve that which in any respect will end in oblivion. Emilie's work is, perhaps, the only thing that justifies my now outstayed, outlived, residence here; but in my defence I will declare that I have not remained through my own will. Here I watch the world I once knew to be full of promise turn pale and insipid, like one who looks out the window and is surprised by dusk, unable now to distinguish things, nor even to see the great shadows that replace them.

No, it is not the will of survival, but the need to finish those duties that are left unfinished.

II

Yet I don't want to talk about myself, but about death, or, I should say, about the order of death in our family.

When they buried little Gil, dressed in his sailor's suit and laid out in his small white coffin, Emilie was unable to rise from her bed, Ned suffered a violent attack that night, and my brother's face transformed into a sort of plaster mask, something roughly modelled on his features of before, but which gave him a rigid, sketchy expression like that of a man already dead, like a man who, if he had once known how to laugh, had now abandoned the intention of ever laughing again.

Help them, perhaps? Help Emilie get over her pain? Help Susan in her infinite suffering of the survivor? Help Austin return to his life, to his convictions, to the love that he once had for his family? But how, through what means, if all he yearned for was to die, to follow his Gilbert?

In that way, like a punishment that has to be borne, the winter of 1884 arrived.

Emilie was not back on her feet until the beginning of March. She spent those months suffering immobility and nausea, until little by little she could walk again, move back to the kitchen, make her jellies, sit in her rocking chair by the window to read her books and to write her letters.

She seemed almost happy, telling me that she was going to recover completely, that Doctor Bigellow's diagnosis had been nothing more than a bad dream.

This spring of hers lasted less than a week. News of Lord's second stroke, this time far more serious than the first, left her as if suspended in time, as if waiting for someone or something to cut the delicate thread of hope that connected her to the only real possibility of love that she had ever had. Well, that something arrived two days later, in a letter sealed with black wax sent by Abbey Farley. I remember Emilie opening it, trembling, whiter than the paper itself, ripping open the seal. "My dear Phillip," she managed to say, before her eyes filled with tears and she couldn't go on. Too weak even for the relief of grief, she asked me with an exhausted gesture to take her to her room.

She lost consciousness while Tom carried her up the stairs.

My sister's body seemed like that of a fawn shot down in the midst of the forest, a tiny animal that had not had the time to learn to resist or to escape, nor even aware of where this cruel blow has come from. Wilting against the strong protecting body of Tom, with one arm dangling at his side, the letter slipped from her fingers.

That is how I learnt that Judge Otis Lord had died without pain.

III

From then on, the only thing that remained strong in my sister was the illness itself, a stench upon her breath that ravaged her from inside, in the manner of worms ravaging the dead buried in the naked earth. Periods of paralysis were interspersed with periods of mental seizures that utterly disabled her, so much so that I can no longer recall Emilie in the kitchen, for example, or anywhere else that wasn't the narrow bed of her room.

One May morning the reaping angels of the soul returned. They had visited us before, a number of times, and they had relaxed their duty because my sister's soul had not been ready to depart, even when her body had decided to long before. But now the fruit was ready to be harvested, about to fall from the branch. The angels danced their white dance stirring up the air around them, until the wind of death came and plucked the fruit from its weakened stem. Ever so carefully the angels gathered it in their wings and flew off with it.

This is how I have always described the day that Emilie died.

IV

One thing for sure is that I've not been able to reconstruct in my memory the exact moment of her death. I know that I was with her – I know *that* as surely as I know my own name – but I cannot manage to see beyond the shroud of fog that surrounds the final days of her life.

A horrible dream, however, torments my nights, nights that are by now woefully shortened by the insomnia of old age, and sleep that is lightened by my endless battles with ghosts. I dream about the precise moment of Emilie's death, unless, that is, my memory has placed a trap there instead of the real event, making me believe that I had never been there at all. Or perhaps it is merely to convince me, with the passage of time, that things have really been just like my memory claims they were. I know that my memory is deceiving me, of course I know, but memory demands an inevitable and private complicity that does nobody any harm. In any respect I am not upset with this: people have demanded my complicity for far more shameful matters than to give credit to a dream.

There is one thing I do remember, with an almost unnatural clarity: my sister's funeral. Nobody in Amherst has gone nor will go, for many years, to a funeral as exquisite as the one Sue and I arranged for Emilie. That is because God, that day, was happy to have her at His side, and this was reflected in every gesture, every almost imperceptible feature of the world.

In the early morning the rains of the night had risen into a thick fog, and the suffocating damp heat heralded a day that would be more than unpleasant. And yet, surprisingly, around midday a fresh, dry breeze picked up from the north, sweeping away the clouds, the fog and the damp, and leaving us with a diaphanous blue sky, and a crystalline air impregnated with the aroma of so many May flowers. Had she been able to – so well did I know her – I know that my sister would have ordered her body to be cremated at the seashore at dawn, like in those ancient Roman funerals, allowing her ashes to be dispersed by the four winds. The sea was far from Amherst, to be sure, but we did have in its stead the Connecticut River, magnificent in the summer, swollen with the meltwaters, and a green valley of corn, oat and wide tobacco leaves.

She was laid out as if she were playing. We had dressed her in a white cotton chemise with plain collar and cuffs, something that Emilie would surely have worn to the funeral of a loved one had she been one to enjoy funerals. Her instructions had been very clear and precise: nobody who had not known her in life could see her in death. In this way, some women who had been childhood friends, Colonel Higginson and family, and the servants of the early years and the present, were the only ones to be granted access to the room where she was laid out in a white coffin. With her straight coppery hair free of adornments and her complexion smooth and serene after so long in bed and so much pain, Emilie seemed young again. She seemed a rare and delicate creature held timelessly in the white vapours of death and eternity; her expression peaceful, almost smiling, and her hands gently crossed over her breast.

After everyone had wished her goodbye with a kiss to her forehead or a touch of her pale hands, I ordered the lid of the coffin to be closed and sealed. Before it was done I had the joy of placing in her hands two heliotropes, fresh and open like two astonished eyes, for Judge Lord. Although I quietly said to her, "These heliotropes are to take to Judge Lord from me," I remember that some of those present turned to look at me with concerned expressions that I chose not to dispel with explanations. In any respect I was not expecting forgiveness from my sister, nor redemption through this gesture. Reverend Jenkins then read some verses from the Scriptures over the closed coffin, and the Colonel recited with his resonant and deep voice a poem by Emily Brontë on immortality.

> No coward soul is mine,
> No trembler on the world's storm-troubled sphere;
> I see the Heaven's glories shine
> And faith shines equal, arming me from fear.

Afterwards, six local workmen, strong Irishmen who had served the family on occasions, bore the coffin effortlessly. Emilie had been precise about this, too, saying that they must be men of the earth, used to working with the earth

– neither family nor functionary nor friend could carry her body. Neither could her body be borne out through the front door, as usual, but through the back door to the yard, without grand ceremony and without affecting the daily affairs in the street.

And that is how it was: we proceeded slowly, forming a solemn congregation behind the coffin, as far as the cemetery. The sun shone with an impertinence that must have delighted Emilie with its stark contrast to the scene of mourning that our dark clothes painted, giving us the appearance of a dark shadow that shamed the life at our feet – the bluebells, wild geraniums, lilies of the valley, heliotropes, violets, and some tiny white flowers like pansies or verbenas that appeared that day as we proceeded to the cemetery, and that I have never seen since.

We buried you in the earth beneath that splendid sun. Father and Mother were at your side, paying vigil, each beneath their respective grey stone that reads no more than their names, like yours, and the year of death. It was strange to come face to face with that year, 1886, engraved upon your stone. It no longer seems strange, that year is now consigned to the distant past, but as the earth was falling, definitively, over your small white coffin – like a child's coffin, scarcely any different from little Gilbert's – the whole ceremony suddenly struck me as being a sort of joke, a nonsense. Or was it your death that had no sense? For if indeed you and I were no longer young, and although the end was always to be expected, you had been conquered by life, not by death. Or perhaps it was, on the contrary, the fact of surviving you that provoked that feeling of unreality throughout the funeral service and the burial. It wasn't that I didn't believe you were dead, that we were interring your body, rather that I could not understand myself, there, in that place – I, Lavinia Dickinson – surrounded by flowers, dressed in black, solemn and motionless as a crow, still breathing, still standing – still breathing...

That same feeling returned some days later, when I entered your room to clean, opening the windows, and I discovered that the same sun, just as insolent as before, was still shining in the sky as it shone at the cemetery, far from death, magnificent, on that spring day of the funeral, absolute and radiant. A sun that I had utterly forgotten.

We buried you silently, I watched some folk throw lilies over the freshly dug earth, then I walked slowly back to the house holding the arms of Maggie and Austin. When I opened the door the first thing I saw was the empty flight of stairs, that stairway that for some time now you had not used because of your illness, and so it seemed almost natural to walk into the house without seeing you. No reason to have expected to see you, seeing as you never inhabited "the strangers' sector", as you used to call the parlour. But when I walked towards the dining room and saw the other stairway, that of the North-East Passage, that secret umbilical corridor that linked your world to ours and that was scarcely more than a discreet collection of steps, I felt how your invisible presence had always illuminated it; and later, when you knew that you would never again walk that corridor, you had charged Maggie with keeping alight the two kerosene lamps during the day.

And yet, this time, when I walked towards the dining room, it was in darkness. A darkness as black as the crow's costume that I was wearing.

You were no longer there, neither the light of your invisible presence, nor that of your lamps, nor that of your candles as you would flee the unannounced arrival of some visitor, either to your bedroom or to the time-honoured vantage point of the top steps. No, you were no longer there, neither had Maggie remembered her duty. Nothing more than an empty stairway, a useless nook dreamed up by a family that had ceased to exist a long time ago.

It was then that I was introduced to the solitude of death, that is nothing more than the solitude of those who remain living. And this was all that was left for me.

10

The Dream

Presentiment is that long shadow on the lawn
Indicative that Suns go down.

— E. Dickinson

I

The dream recurs; it has recurred since then like a premonition.

I am seated in the rocking chair in Emilie's room. I know that my sister is in a state of profound unconsciousness, swept away in a dream from which she will never return. I know, because Doctor Bigellow had diagnosed it a long while before, that this slow illness was intent on patiently eating away at her insides, and that there was nothing to be done.

The rocking chair breaks the silence with a persistent, almost complaining creak against the wooden floor. Emilie's room is in darkness, the windows shut. I know that she is not going to awaken, that I am alone in the room; and I also know that I am awaiting the moment of her death, the end of so much misery, so much powerlessness. I know all of this in the way we know things in dreams, irrefutably, despite what reason and waking may tell us.

Emilie is propped up on some pillows, the only position that grants her a little air into her tired lungs. Within her breast is a black machine that I can see through the translucent skin that covers the skeletal bars of her ribcage, a machine like a clockwork motor, only black, unoiled and creaky. It sometimes stops for a few seconds until some mysterious force sets the cogs in motion again, meshing together unevenly, uncoupling, breaking with the friction. With each revolution a dreadful sound is forced from my sister's mouth – it is the slow grinding of this black machine that keeps her alive, or at least breathing. But I can do nothing to help her. I can do nothing but keep on rocking in the old rocking chair, its creaking against the floor keeping time to her dying breaths: she stops I stop, she breathes I resume my rocking.

Suddenly she stops breathing for a minute, and Doctor Bigellow, disguised as Father, enters the room without knocking and says: "chloroform and olive oil."

He repeats, looking at me, "chloroform and olive oil."

"What for?" I ask.

"Joints," he replies blankly.

"Leave her in peace. Please go."

Now it is Austin who looks at me from the gaze of Doctor Bigellow. Where is the real doctor? In the last few months Emilie has not wanted to see him, nor to have anything to do with his medicines. And now it is Austin who pours a green liquid over the broken machine.

"Leave her!" I cry more urgently, but Austin ignores me and continues to pour oil over her. The machine then starts winding and grinding again, and I start rocking again. A few minutes pass and the machine stops for the second time. It is just before six in the afternoon. Through the window a little insipid light enters – the wan light of cloudy afternoons. From the bed, her eyes at once open and, sparkling, Emilie looks at me. She gestures feebly with her hand for me to approach.

"Don't think that I'm going away, Vinnie. Think more that I am going home."

A black breath then floats from her mouth, and she breathes no more.

I lightly touch her cheeks that have begun to grow cold, as if they had been cold for a long while and that meagre breath had been a lie so as to hold her back. Cold lips, gypsy lips, open eyes, opaque like walnuts. Everything about her is dead. There is nothing poetic about it, nothing luminous, piteous, celestial. There is no God here. I remember my dream, perhaps there is no God anywhere, and this is the most definite farewell.

From outside comes the clear siren of the factory, as it does at six every afternoon, and I hear it also in my dream. I take Emilie's hand and discover that on her index finger there is an ink stain.

I awaken still feeling her hand in mine, but I open my eyes in the darkness of dawn, and the wall of my room returns nothing to me but the grey nothingness of its ruin. Grief overwhelms me, as if it were I who were dying.

Emilie, dear Emilie, my Emilie. How can I go about my life if you are not with me?

II

From that day, that dream has become the presage that the angels of death will visit, or that they have just left with their weightless burden – such is a soul – wrapped in their wings.

This morning I awoke with a peculiar feeling, unsettling, frightening, but at the same time fatal, as if I knew that I could do nothing more than suffer and become sad. Soon enough I found the reason: Baboo Junior, my pretty, frolicky little Baboo Junior, was dead in the kitchen, lying still warm by the oven, his body like a tiny Bengal tiger resting against the iron wall as if it had needed that small warmth to resist death a while longer. Maggie had not touched him, but she had definitely seen him. She knows. She knows well enough.

While I looked in the garden for a suitable place to bury him, I recall that whenever one of my tribe of pussy cats died or disappeared, Emilie would always try to convince me that cats were really immortal, beyond the story of their nine lives and other such nonsense. For her the ideal cat must have a rat in its teeth, as that was the only service that they gave. That was also the only reason she could tolerate them. Forgive me – that and the fact that I loved them. This was the same respect with which I tolerated for my part the dogs that Emilie usually gathered around her, dirty, noisy and stupid.

Next to the grave of Baltazar, the last of old Quincey's clan, I buried Baboo Junior with the help of the gardener. Well, in truth it was he who buried the dear cat, but I dictated the exact spot, and I had brought him there wrapped in a tattered shawl upon which the poor little thing used to sleep.

III

Keats, the birds, and the old iron Franklin stove remind me of my sister, just like trees and paintings remind me of Austin, and heliotropes and the smell of soap of Mother. Of Father – alas – almost everything reminds me of him, even my own gestures.

The corners of this house have their own names, they are not innocent. I go from one to the next like someone wandering around the graves of a cemetery, where each stone declares the name of a loved one, or at least a friend, and where the spirits have a friendly texture that invites conversation. I know that those spirits do not dwell in this house, and I know that the ghost that surprises Maggie each morning with the arranged kitchen utensils is no more than the illusion that I often create; and I also know that none of those spirits, if I know them well, would ever cling again with such passion to the objects of this life.

Yes, I know and understand the matter perfectly. But it so happens that the dark corners of this house do not age, whereas I do. I can no longer see clearly Father's face, but I can see his austere expression, the hard line of his lips. I can see Austin's curly red hair when he was young and would write those passionate love letters to Sue – not his vacuous, absent eyes at the end of his life. Yet I cannot even see Emilie's face – that face "that had not a single good feature", as Higginson said to various people, including Mabel. It is not so, Emilie was beautiful in a way that is difficult to describe, and even harder to recall with precision.

A while ago I was asked for a photograph, a portrait of her, any available image for the second edition of her poems, avoiding that frightful portrait of the three of us as children, with those suffocating dresses and consumptive eyes. I searched in vain, knowing full well that I hadn't a single photograph of my sister, but finally I did find just the one, the only one that she had allowed to be taken of her, when she was sixteen. So serious and pale and thin, her hair combed and parted at the middle and pulled back, the dark neckline of her dress, all so solemn. So different, this Emilie, so distant! She never again arranged her hair in this way – her hair was red and wavy, naturally rebellious, utterly unlike mine, which was straight and dark. She would wear her hair long, perhaps tied up with a ribbon, and the curls would escape over her face, impossible to control, giving her an untidy, childish appearance. Sometimes she wouldn't even tie it back, and then, quite categorically, she resembled a goblin. I would say to her, "Emilie, what *do* you

look like!" and she would always answer me, "the same as I
have since birth, unless, of course, I was born with my hair
in a bun", and she would carry on as before with her hair
loose as the wind.

In any respect, scarcely anyone ever saw her beyond
Maggie, Sue, the children, and Austin, and eventually some childhood friend or favourite neighbour whom
Emilie would perchance consent to receive at home, or because she was, for example, in the kitchen making toffee
and felt curious about the conversation, or because she
felt compelled through pity to buy something from some
itinerant salesman who had come to the back door with
baskets laden with indescribable wares. Maggie would
hide these charitable purchases in the basement so that
I wouldn't find them and raise the roof, as she would say.
Since she came to this house, Maggie has often exaggerated
things, like all the Irish, as well as being stubborn.

In truth, though, I was always quite amused by Emilie's
purchases, especially when she would tell me about her
encounters with the salesmen or women who would
approach expecting to find me or Maggie, who had precise
instructions in this matter. To overcome the obstinate
resistance that experience had taught them to expect,
they always came resolved to extol the most extraordinary
virtues of the most extraordinary products; and then
suddenly... they would find themselves face to face with
my sister, my sister who was unknown to them, who, as
far as they knew, could have been dead, a ghost dressed
in white, a weeping nun, a madwoman shut away in the
house, a unexplained myth, as nobody ever knew exactly
why Emily Dickinson was considered in this way. And so
they would all of a sudden find themselves before Emilie,
who would be wearing a large headscarf and a shawl
over her dress, with her hands covered in flour, jelly or

cinnamon, and a violet pencil behind her ear. Some would stand dumb, unable even to utter an apologetic greeting. Others would hasten to show her what they had brought in their baskets with such zeal – originally destined for Maggie or me – that Emilie would succumb like a moth to a candle flame, unable to determine whether the goods were really necessary or not, but believing unconditionally the explanations that these wretches had tuned to this purpose. Others, a few, would remember Emilie as a little girl and would tell her anecdotes about the family, above all about Father, and my sister would end up buying out of pity; and she might even, if there were children, hand them chocolates and flowers. At the end of the day she would tell me her "adventures" and would show me her useless treasures: a couple of cameos of false coral, a liquid to kill cockroaches, an instrument supposedly manufactured by Indians whose purpose we never figured out, if, indeed, it was designed for any purpose at all...

"What are we going to do with all this?" I would ask, dazed by a drawer overflowing with fruits of a hard, opalescent shell, brought from some remote place, impossible both to classify and to eat.

"I don't know, Vinnie, but the woman had the most delightful daughter, who seemed to adore my new cookies."

"Did she tell you at least how to cook them? How to cut them open? How to store them?"

"No, in fact she never did. Perhaps we can make a jelly out of them? What do you think, Vin?"

IV

Yes, the Emilie who showed herself to the occasional salesman was closer to the real Emilie than this rigid

photograph. She hated photographs. She hated her own
image, I've no idea why. From the moment that she
declared that her gypsy face was for ever, she no longer
cared what she looked like, nor did she allow anyone ever
to paint her portrait. In part it was that, certainly, but in
part it was also that Emilie greatly enjoyed her extravagant
fame as an inaccessible and unknown figure. That is why
she dressed in white.

How is it possible that so much excitement has been
generated by something as basic as my sister's clothes?
Emilie began to dress in white because she liked clear tones
and because she had no interest in choosing from different
colours every day. The same was true with textures, and for
that reason, besides being white, the fabric was piqué in
summer and merino wool in winter. On occasions a shawl
or a cape over her shoulders, or a headscarf if she was in
the garden. Her dresses, which were all the same save a
slight variety of pleat or cuff or flare, were made by Miss
D., who made them for me, although she knew they were
for Emilie. Why have people made such a fuss over this?
Nobody has noticed, for example, that whereas my sister
always dressed in white, I, for a number of years now, have
exclusively worn black. Nor that Austin always wore hats
that were three times bigger than normal.

When I was asked for Emilie's portrait, I took this one
to Mrs Graves, who herself had sought the help of a paint-
er of miniatures, Laura Hill. Between the two of them
they modified my sister's solemn and pallid expression,
softening the curve of the lips, touching up the dull tone of
the cheeks, adding the curls that fell about her face. They
also painted in the small ivory and gold brooch that Emilie
used to wear at her breast. This new modified portrait has
more of her than any other; and I left orders for Higginson,
and stated in my will, that only this portrait should be used

for the next edition and all subsequent editions. Emilie would not have accepted it, but she would not have accepted anything, perhaps not even the publication itself, nor talk about retouched photographs. Austin can no longer make any comment on the matter, and Sue has expressed her approval of the miniature. Mattie also says that she remembers her like this. For me, to see her unkempt and wavy hair again has been more than enough.

$\mathcal{V}$

I have left the portrait in the display cabinet in the dining room, perhaps too solemn a spot, to be honest, yet from time to time Ned or Maggie catch me talking to her about some fatal accident or other. I either play dumb or I stare at them with my old madwoman's face, until they get scared and run off to tell Sue. I imagine that Sue, who understands how things are, smiles and tells them to leave Aunt Vinnie alone with her ghosts and her spirits. It is a custom of mine, or at least it was, as deep-rooted as my love of the macabre or Emilie's predisposition for laughing at me and at those who waste time writing such newspaper articles. We would usually do it like this: I would read her the most gruesome pieces, those that had the most morbid descriptions or those that reported the greatest number of casualties, and she would pass her comments, interrupting me so that in my total absorption the thing wouldn't disturb us too much. Now, whenever I come across an article like that I read it to her, and I can rest assured that her ghost, wherever it may be, still replies in the same way as before.

"Listen to this, Emilie. Leave that enormous book for a moment and pay attention to the story of this poor man: 'The body of an unknown man...'"

"Only the body… otherwise they would have said who the poor soul was…"

"'…was found late last night suspended' (listen to that – literally hanging) 'from the engine of train number 31…'"

"What a horrible number."

"'…that covers the route from Boston to Albany, before reaching Palmer.'"

"Before reaching Palmer? How could they have found him if the train was moving?"

"That's coming… 'The train is an express that carries mail, and it does not stop at Palmer.' Emilie, I'm only telling you what it says in the newspaper. 'As the train was coming into the town…'"

"Here comes the blood…"

"'…the electric flash of lightning lit up the front of the engine, and the guard discovered the body hanging between the metal bars at the front of the train.'"

"Good gracious, what a horrendous spectacle! That poor guard cannot have slept since then."

"'It has not been established where it was that the man was struck by the train.'"

"But of course the mangled state of the body doesn't make the assessment any easier. It would be easier if at least there were different types of vegetation along the route."

"'The body is that of a man of around fifty years of age…'"

"So young, Vinnie, younger than us…"

"'…five foot ten.'"

"With those dimensions he could have slipped through the bars!"

"'He did not wear a beard.'"

"And who's interested in that?"

"'A scar on the left cheek, a cut on the right ear and several teeth missing from the upper jaw.'"

"Well at least we know that the body has kept the left cheek, the right ear and the upper jaw, which is something at least."

"'He was wearing grey trousers, a dark jacket and a blue shirt with white stripes.'"

"Surely a Boston banker who has suffered an amorous disappointment."

"'...he also wore a pair of leather boots in good condition. The man's neck was broken, as were several ribs, the left thigh bone had been severed, and the hip...'"

"Vinnie, please, this is making me nauseated."

"I'm nearly at the end. 'Doctor Holbrook, the forensic surgeon, examined the body after it was delivered to the authorities of Palmer.'"

"It should have been delivered directly to the cemetery, let the poor fellow rest in peace once and for all."

"Poor man, Emilie, it makes me feel so sad. Do you not feel sad? First to be left hanging all night from the train, then dragged around the streets of Palmer...'

"Lord – may this man return to the earth from whence he came."

"Amen."

"Amen."

11

The Publication

A word is dead when it is said,
Some say.
I say it just begins to live
That day.

– E. Dickinson

I

*T*he year that Emilie died was also the year that Austin and Mabel's *affaire* was on the lips of everyone in town. Before this it had been no more than an irritating whisper, an indiscreet and tactless comment that I would have heard uttered by one of those matronly ladies at those stupid gatherings which, thanks to God, I had not attended for a long while. Mindless gossip that nobody, save Sue, paid any attention to. She would take it to heart, observing it every day in the pained expression of her son, in the sly conversations between servants, and in those furtive exchanges that most humiliated her between friends running into each other at the market, in the street, or in the safety of a society reunion or college event – words offered with the delight and glee of those who never suffer their meaning in the flesh, by those who would clumsily break off their speech upon seeing Sue arrive and start up some banal conversation in sickly sweet and vaguely compassionate tones that did no more than betray the prior nastiness. Sue was not stupid, quite the contrary, and her heart always suspected more than it should.

One afternoon we were at the Evergreens, sitting around the fireplace. Austin, Mattie and Ned were also there. At one particular moment Austin, who had been lazily reading in the leather armchair, saw something in the newspaper that caught his attention and at once began to comment on it out loud to Ned. The piece in question was some nonsense about a murder committed by a circus artist on the coast of California, a case that had been talked about considerably those months. I, intrigued by such excitement, asked Austin what it was that interested him so much in that infamous story. But before Austin could respond, Sue – from her own armchair and with a violence and bitterness that stunned me, and which later I regretted not having fully fathomed in time – said:

"Leave him, Vinnie! Let him be with his newspaper. It's a blessing to know that he is interested in *something*."

Austin did not even register, and Ned and Mattie looked at her astonished, but saying nothing. After a while Austin got up and left.

I did not want to ask on that occasion, nor on others in which Sue let fly with similar remarks, and I now regret it. I suppose that both Emilie and I preferred to believe that Austin was incapable of betraying Sue in this so... disgusting way. Emilie more than anyone had taken sides with Austin, and thanks to this extreme loyalty – a far too precious and wasteful gesture – the final years of her relationship with Sue were strained and difficult. Sue no longer wrote to her like before, and she now scarcely ever came over to the house. Emilie herself began to suffer ever more greatly after Gilbert, while Sue, bearing the pain of death and the more complex pain of betrayal, tried to distance herself from the town, heading off to the coast of Maine with her children whenever she was able. The ungrateful wretch that was my brother left her to her own desires, which for him meant more free space for his deception.

Some months after Mother's funeral, Mabel and her husband David moved into a wooden house that they christened "Dell", just a few yards from the Evergreens and from this house. In fact, the plot that the house was built upon was the furthest section of the Dickinson land, property of my Father. Austin had given it to them, without consulting us, because it was part of his own inheritance.

Following various comings and goings, pardons, apologies, and repeated incidences, the Todds were in the end not welcome at Sue's house. For Austin it was the perfect excuse to arrange assiduous visits to their house, where, besides, it was said that other young women were invited by David, while Mabel played the perfect and generous hostess.

My brother, Mabel and David were known as the triumvirate. How repugnant I now find these sordid details.

And yet, I've still made no mention of the worst, ashamed as I am by my own stupidity, my own faithfulness, as childish and useless as Emilie's. Yes, I've not yet mentioned the worst, and perhaps it's because most of that sinful event occurred right here, before our eyes, in the safety of this house, where Father and Mother had lived, where Austin had sworn his love to Sue, where Emilie died, where his children have played. And where I live – I, who still deserve his respect. In this house they consummated their relationship. Heaven knows how many times they locked themselves in one of the bedrooms. I cannot conceive of a more hideous situation nor of a greater lack of respect on the part of my brother and that woman, she who dared to come here to play the piano and sing those precious songs before unashamedly rolling herself into bed here in this house. In *my* house. For I am a Dickinson, as much as Emilie and he, and this house is my house. I live here and

I bear its sadness. Have I not the right to know what goes on within these four walls?

Ah, such a clumsy claim! Such a mistake! Above all for Austin, seeing as the rights that he had were nothing more than his whims and his tremendous selfishness.

"I have a right to be happy! I have a right to make the woman I love happy!" he cried at the top of his voice that afternoon that he confessed the whole truth to me – well, he couldn't keep it hidden any longer – and ordered me – no, not a request or an appeal, but an order – to carry out through my own will that which he, cowardly dog that he was, was unable to do.

This happened a long time after Emilie's funeral, when Austin himself was at death's door without anyone knowing it. A lapse of nearly ten years separates the deaths of my sister and my brother, during which time I fought like the devil himself to achieve that which has kept me going to this very day: to grant Emily Dickinson the place she deserves in the canon of great literature of this country.

II

From the afternoon in which I found the first of the boxes that contained Emilie's poems, an anxiety that I cannot explain compelled me to spend the hours and then the days that ensued searching every last hidden corner of the house for more of those boxes, until I found a wooden box in Maggie's trunk, a place that appears to have been chosen by my sister to hide her treasures. Thenceforth, for a long time, I devoted myself to voracious reading, as if those papers held the key to all the secrets of my life. I could not stop reading and rereading them, untying and retying them in the same precise way that Emilie had left them, smoothing them against my skirt, folding them, spreading them out across the dining-room table. I compared one with the next, I scrutinized them, contemplating them beyond the mere words, as if they were objects that awaited a sign, a mysterious password, to come to life.

For there, in those verses written in so many different styles of hand, was Emily Dickinson, someone I've never completely known. Who was Emily, therefore? A stranger, a ghost who had little in common with that red-haired ghost who appeared in the kitchen to arrange the spoons that Maggie purposefully left in disarray. An exile from the world who had written thousands of poems throughout her life, most of them brief, visceral, incomprehensible, small like children, that she had looked after jealously, away from prying eyes, without leaving a single pointer, a single trail towards them.

I must confess that anger and perturbation dominated my soul as much as wonder and stupor during those hours that I spent watching over the table covered in poems, as if the summer breeze could enter through the window and take them from me. There was nothing from my sister with respect to these poems, neither instruction nor concrete reference. Burning them would have been the correct thing to do, I suppose, what anyone else in my position would have done. Make a huge fire with them in an old stone vessel in the garden, as people usually do with the correspondence of the recently dead. Let the earth and the air be the only ones to know. I must confess that I was about to do this. Why did she tell me nothing about her legacy of poems? Why did she spend her entire life beneath the same roof as I, only to die without having ever revealed what was hidden in those boxes? Why not even one word of guidance, or at least of explanation?

Because it is easier to let the weight of what you've been

unable to resolve fall upon someone else's shoulders, upon that person who has not been prevented by death from resolving the matter. In this way, those unresolved decisions fell upon me. I, the faithful zealot who will live or die sorrowfully, who will or will not pay for having done right or wrong. Who knows?

Those decisions that could have brought me the greatest grief were bequeathed to me by my brother and sister. I am not attempting to explain my anger so much as to pardon my actions, because it is my actions that have brought judgement upon me, not that fury of love for them that I have felt like a faithful parasite, nor the pain of my soul, which is too private – no, just my actions.

But this is no longer important. This is all no more than the bitterness that I will take with me to my grave.

It was when I was looking at my sister's poems – wild children raised in a wild garden – that I came across the key for reading them. It was also through reading them out loud, one by one, that I discovered how to understand something of them. The density, the rare quality of the words, and that impossible cadence is not to be found in the rhyme – often absent – but in the vast whole, in the sum of all, as if they had been created to be grouped in infinite ways, forming a continuity, an evolving rhythm. And it is this greater rhythm, the only rhythm that I could perceive in the poems, that constituted the magic quality, never until then perceived in any other poet.

I could not judge like a critic or a well-versed writer whether the poems were good, bad or average, whether they could be placed within a particular genre of what people were reading at that time, whether shades of Shakespeare or the Brontës or Browning were clear to see, whether they were pretentious, forced or sublime. For me, someone who has never cared unduly for poetry, they were cryptic, utterly indecipherable beyond the obvious meaning of the individual words, or beyond one or two simple, brief poems like nursery rhymes. Individually, the poems reflected the world of that stranger I described earlier, of that creature who dwelt here with me and whom, through her excessive fear or self-sufficiency, I never knew. I only know that I experienced no other certainty upon reading them than the magic that burst from all of them together.

And yet, I cannot fully believe that it was my own certainty, strong as it was, that led me to publish the poems posthumously, to collect together all these verses that had been scattered throughout the dark corners of our house and the houses of friends, and to exhibit them to the scrutiny of the world. My hands suddenly started to burn. Suddenly I could not bear the idea of being alone with this Emilie that I never knew. Suddenly I felt the need to display her as she herself had wanted to be, to immortalize her in her own words, to give her voice its necessary, indisputable destiny. Suddenly the poems transformed themselves into a sort of duty of love, because there was no other way I could rid myself of them. I had adopted them, just like I would have adopted her children, and I resolved to devote what was left of my life to her poor orphans.

I knew that by taking the reins of this legacy I would be forging the destiny of a stranger.

III

I would rather not weigh down my spirit with these memories, but it is inevitable: they are dark visitors who call at my door on a daily basis, and I know that by trying to ignore them I'm only forcing them to remain in the shadows, preying on my conscience, awaiting the right moment to pounce. I've now resigned myself to this, and now prefer to attend to them with a certain deference, as one ought to attend to long-standing enemies, in order to avoid direct confrontation.

The first person to whom I turned to seek help in the task of compiling the poems was, naturally, Susan. Who else was there who could understand Emilie, my sister, as much as she could understand Emily, the poet? Who if not Sue could appreciate with fairness the quality of the verse, and could select out of the hundreds and hundreds of poems that I had discovered the most brilliant ones? Which other person in this town possessed such an intimate knowledge of literature at the same time as understanding the eccentric personality of Emilie?

I waited for her for nearly two years, after sending her a box containing more than seven hundred poems and other new fascicles that I found nestling in the most unlikely places of the house. I know that during this time Sue sent various poems, those that she considered best or simply the most accessible to the public, to a variety of journals, and that one by one the editors rejected the submissions. Too odd, they said, too eloquent, too anarchic, too short. Too Emily. But that was precisely what prevented Sue, unlike anyone else in her place, from surrendering.

One day she sent for me to tell me that she had now given up trying to publish the works officially, saying that it would be more advisable "to avoid criticism" to think about a single, home-made edition of poems and letters, which would remain in the town, destined not for the general public but for those who had shared any intimacy with Emilie. Without bothering even to look further into the details of this venture, and considering it an unworthy solution for my sister, I urged Sue to return to me all the poems. She tried to hold me back, offering me vague arguments as to why she had reached her conclusion, but it was quite clear to the two of us that she neither could nor would confess her true motives. For my part, blinded by the urgency of so much time already lost, I ignored her advice and her reasoning, and left her.

Had I considered a little closer her desire to avoid criticism, I would perhaps have understood something of her behaviour, and I could have waited for the storm to pass, without pressurizing her, until she took up the job again on her own behalf. But no, her negativity after all those months angered me tremendously, and in my anger I could only think about doing that which I would later regret so much: approach the only other person who was capable of such a task, if not because of her knowledge of Emilie, then at least for her general knowledge of the world.

And so in this way I played myself into the hands of Mabel Loomis Todd, the woman who at that time figured in every piece of gossip and tattle as the lover of my brother, she who had tormented Sue's nights, she who I, in my stubborn folly, now entwined irredeemably in the destiny both of Emily and of all the family.

IV

Before anything else, copies needed to be made of an overwhelming quantity of poems. This, in my opinion, was the hardest task. Several people I know have asked me, if the task consisted in only copying, transcribing methodically in black ink each original onto spotless paper, without amendments, why did I not carry out the task myself. I smile to myself; the simple answer is that they have never had to suffer my horrendous calligraphy in the flesh. Spiders on the paper, Joseph used to call it; Chinese characters, according to Austin. Amongst my close friends there was a long-standing joke:

"Vinnie Dickinson has written to me."

"Ah – and what does the letter say?"

"No idea."

It would have been useless, at least its only use would have been to make things worse. I needed a mountain of poems to be copied out intelligibly, or better still copied out upon one of those new writing machines, with the plan of sending them eventually to an editor, thus keeping the originals in my possession. Moreover, I needed someone astute and sensitive enough to be able to decide which might be the correct word out of the various alternative words that Emilie would usually jot down – some humbled by successive correction, others highlighted, underlined or confined to the margins as if waiting for the appropriate moment to be inserted in the precise place allocated to them. Beyond this, I needed someone to determine the accuracy of the dates that she would write or not according to her mood, and that rendered impossible any attempt to order them chronologically – if indeed chronology or any system of ordering *could* have any sense with that crowd of wild poems.

For this job, therefore, it was absolutely imperative to find someone whose knowledge of literature was greater than mine, especially with regard to poetry, a genre that I've never approached without feeling like a thief, always through the darkest door, scarcely with time enough to grab what I can fit in my bag and run off before being discovered with this booty that should not belong to me. I am well aware of my weaknesses and I know how to recognize virtues in others that I myself lack, therefore I considered Sue the ideal candidate, but owing to her amazing delay and her negative conclusion, I decided that Mabel Todd, who had striven uselessly to be worthy of the personal attention of Emily, was next on my list of possible candidates.

Mabel was the star of Amherst in the best and the worst of senses: she travelled, painted, sang, played the piano, took part in gatherings, organized *soirées*, and met of course almost daily with Austin, in such a way that she had little time to spare. I had to insist on my proposal until she accepted.

She began half-heartedly, working irritatingly slowly, but she had a machine for typing that made the task easier and produced neat copies in strong and durable black ink. I pursued her, stirring her on with flattery to compel her to get through the poems, and when she arrived at the house I would prepare her stimulating punches with whiskey, white sugar and egg that could have raised the dead from the tomb.

Finally she finished the job. It was now three years since Emilie's funeral.

About this time, when Colonel Higginson paid an untimely visit to Amherst for the annual meeting of a philanthropic society, I begged him to come and see me. That is how I first showed him the few originals of Emilie's work that Mabel had been returning to me, arranged like an exotic quilt on the dining-room table, and I recited them to him, striving to capture that mysterious rhythm of the collection. I then offered him the poems to publish, with the determination of someone offering a treasure, without even entertaining the possibility of rejection.

Before taking his leave – the meeting had lasted less than an hour – the Colonel asked me to send the copies to Boston, telling me that he would take charge of writing a preface, and that he would employ all his ability and experience in helping to find an editor for Emilie's work. "Her memory compels me to do so," I remember he said with a solemn expression as he took his leave.

With this initial promise, work soon began on the copies until around six hundred and seventy-four poems were completed. Then, with a trip to Boston owed her, Mabel took the copies in person to Higginson.

I must say, thanks to all those involved, that the happy outcome of all this work was that in November of 1890 the first volume of poetry of Emily Dickinson appeared – "edited by two of her friends, Mabel Loomis Todd & T.W. Higginson" – which was only a half-truth, at least with respect to Mabel. The book at once caused general fascination: not *one* opinion was conciliatory or mediocre, but quite the opposite. Some reviews were full of fervent praise and others wrote it off as an experiment, utterly lacking poetic technique, but withal powerful and necessary, even in the detail of their lack of orthodoxy. The book itself was beautiful, blue leather with golden letters, simple and at the same time imposing, and the ridiculously small print run was sold out in a couple of months, forcing the publishers, with an enthusiasm renewed only by the success, to issue a reprint while calling for new volumes of her poems and letters to be put together.

That success, I deem, was what prompted Mabel's sudden and still lasting fever of activity to gather and copy every last word that had come from Emilie's hand.

Within a few years, news of Emily Dickinson, the Queen Recluse, had filled the bookstores of the state with three volumes of poetry and two volumes of letters. In each volume the name of Mabel appears, despite the fact that I had specified in a letter addressed to Higginson soon before the appearance of the first volume that I wished for her collaboration to be strictly sub rosa. It did not seem to me opportune to explain in a letter the reasons for this. It would have been impossible, besides being an inconvenience, to reveal to the state my relationship with Sue, nor the level of deterioration that my brother's marriage had reached, owing, precisely, to this woman who now implanted her name in golden letters alongside that of my sister. Nor should I have wished to air my own disgust at the excessive and arrogant reactions of Mabel to the verdicts of the critics, as if my participation in the publication of the poems had been so small that it was not even worthy of the merest mention, whereas *her* contribution had been crucial for the flowering of Emilie's talent.

There is no doubt that with the publication of each of these editions under those conditions the distance between me and Sue and my niece and nephew grew ever wider. Curiously, Austin kept himself apart, making degrading comments about my thirst for another's fame, comments which, I hasten to add, were more directed towards comforting his lover than irritating me. I suspect that for my brother, who had always harboured his own, not so secret, artistic desires, this explosive, posthumous, rise to fame of Emily must have preyed on his nerves. Poor Austin, by that stage he had abandoned himself to the miseries of his soul, and nothing now mattered to him save his escapades with Mabel, his dealings with worthless objects of art, or planting trees all over Amherst. He was old and tired of living this double life, of looking at his children's eyes with a guilt that he could not ignore, and that was eating away at his soul.

And if I had managed up till that point to ignore the rumours, it was Austin who took it upon himself, without the slightest consideration, to open my eyes. A short while before he finally took to his bed with a sickness of the soul from which he would never recover, he came to see me. It had been quite some time since he had last come by the house, although it is odd to think that I had seen him on an almost daily basis through the window as he would stroll briskly along the edge of the garden on his way to Mabel's house. I welcomed him with a cup of tea, and we spoke alone in the library, so that Maggie would not be able to hear us from the kitchen. There was nothing noble in his voice when he told me that he had loved Mabel for more than ten years, and that were he not bound to his home through his children, he would have left with her a long time ago. Since Gilbert's death nothing mattered to him, and the little life that he had left to enjoy he had decided to enjoy in his own way, whatever anyone might think. For a moment transformed, he shouted he had a right to be happy – I don't know whether to impress me or whether it was the only way he knew of apologizing – as all the while I did nothing but look at him, with neither surprise, pain nor compassion. I looked at this man and scarcely knew him, and this saddened me more than his sordid confession. On the other hand I suppose that I did know his story – I hadn't paid heed to the rumours, I hadn't wanted to pay heed to Sue, but I knew...

Then, before leaving, and offering no explanation, he told me two more things: he was sick, very sick, and he instructed me to cede his part of Father's inheritance to Mabel upon his death. The rest of his personal estate would go to Sue and the children, but everything that came from the Dickinsons and that belonged to him was to be left for Mabel. He didn't wait for my reply, nor, in truth, did he really care. He simply took it as fact that I would carry out his wishes as someone obeying a natural order, just or not.

A week later his heart started to fail. His body, always so strong and healthy, rapidly weakened, and in less than a month, Austin died. He was in his house, lying in his bed, and a sudden and silent attack took him by surprise. Nobody, according to the doctor, could have done anything for him beyond taking his hand and letting him die in peace.

I honestly could not say whether or not my brother would have died in peace. The wake was brief, a vain attempt by Sue to make it discreet and, I suspect, to avoid the presence of Mabel. But Mabel managed to go, alone, entering secretly through the side door of the house thanks to Ned, who had organized the proceedings so that the rest of the family would not even see her. Not one of the Todds, however, came to the funeral. That would have caused a scandal, something Mabel understood perfectly, and the freshness of her treasured "fame" would not permit her such a blunder.

The people of Amherst mourned Austin more than they had Father; the day of his funeral was decreed a day of mourning, all the stores were shut and nearly every neighbour joined the procession to the cemetery. I myself had long mourned his departure in silence, since the day of Gilbert's death, because for me Austin, my brother, the man I knew and loved, had also died on that day.

V

Emilie's final book was the most contentious, in every respect. Mabel had the original poems and the almost finished manuscript in her possession, all that was left was to alter certain details of style that the editor demanded, details that Mabel had never thought to consult me about. It angered me tremendously that they assumed the right of amending the poems, of changing those words that Emily had sought with such care, of clipping verses according to their whim so as to give the illusion of a certain orthodoxy in the rhyme. In doing so they were simply reducing Emily, making her digestible for those who had no real interest in her. These were issues of the market, or of fashion, and although the finished product would be the published volume occupying its allotted place, I could not allow myself to interfere nor demand anything. This is because I held within me the secret hope that one day, in the next century perhaps, someone would take the effort of returning to the intact originals that I still kept. Basically, I let Mabel and the Colonel act freely. And even so, there was still this third, final volume of poems, the volume that had been the hardest to collate and finish, and it was almost ready.

Then, scarcely two months after Austin's death, Mabel appeared at my house to ask me to make effective the order my brother had given concerning the inheritance. That's to say, she came to ask me to hand over to her, which means to the Todds, the inheritance that Father had bequeathed Austin. That shameless individual stood before me dressed from head to toe in black, as she had publicly dressed every day since Austin's death. And she also wore a gold ring, blatant and vulgar, with the letters A and M intertwined. I remember that her eyes were full of tears and her lips quivered and hands trembled when she finally came out with the purpose of her visit.

I had to contain myself from throwing her into the street. And yet, without showing the least emotion, least of all the anger that was burning like fire within, I genially informed her that what Austin had not done himself I myself was powerless to do, for all that he might have said at the end. She must understand the delicate position in which such an act would put me with my own family, that I was terribly sorry, and would she please send my regards to her husband. I stressed the word *husband* in such a way that, to preserve a certain decorum, Mabel changed the subject to Emily's book. With the same control and measure that I had just used, she told me that she was about to send the first manuscript for its initial evaluation. *About to send it*, she stressed, and then left.

Following this conversation, which took place in October 1895, I knew that Mabel would not be happy until she had taken something of the Dickinsons, and that I could not under any circumstances allow myself to be beaten by the nausea that her greed produced, at least not before the book was in print.

But it would be this book, precisely this book, that the leech would use to crush me.

Two months passed with no word of the book. Carefully avoiding talk of Austin's inheritance, I attempted to maintain cordial relations with Mabel, trying to get some information out of her. But she would not say a word, or she would be off for a few days for a conference, or she would simply, and with no subtlety, ignore me. She believed that with this strategy she was going to manipulate me like she had Austin, but she was mistaken.

Predicting that she would not send a single page to the publisher if I did not give her something in exchange, before the year was up I invited her to my house to tell her that I had resolved to fulfil, in part, the promise of my brother: to present to her a plot of land that bordered our property, where Austin himself had planted his trees, and of which both she and her husband had insisted on numerous occasions that no building was to be allowed there that might spoil the view from their own house. It was little compared to what Austin had promised her, even more so seeing as Austin had ordered me to cede it to her as part of her inheritance.

To be honest I did not aspire to keeping Mabel happy with this, only hoping that with the legal transfer she would finish her work on the book. But Mabel was far from stupid, and seeing that I was not to fulfil Austin's request, something that she never expected, she was more alert and on the defensive than ever. In this way, she returned with greater insistency to the matter in hand:

"Vinnie, remember that we must measure carefully the size of that plot of land."

"Vinnie, we must have this deed drawn up, I have with me some blank forms that Austin left, I could..."

"Vinnie, we will need a witness to sign both forms, shall I advise an Amherst lawyer or would you rather find one yourself?"

I replied that she should sort out the paperwork, that she could advise anyone she liked, that she could organize the blasted affair however she wanted, but that *please*, *please*, could she finish the corrections of Emily's book. Far from gaining time, I was burying myself deeper and deeper in promises. Mabel was drowning me with her requests and demands and I was assenting with resignation, with no possibility of escape.

Whom could I turn to? Who was there to give me advice or assistance?

I couldn't even dream of asking Sue, it had been too long since last we had any contact because of those initial books. Ned and Mattie would have taken their mother's side: they detested Mabel and they would have done all they could to make me abandon Emilie's book before ceding anything to her. There was nobody I could talk to regarding Austin's ridiculous promise, as this would have involved admitting what could not be admitted, and would have rekindled the scandal around town.

What could I do? I was utterly alone, at the mercy of the persistent avarice of that woman and the likelihood that greater shame and humiliation would fall upon my family, more even than my brother had caused with his own conduct.

On a number of occasions I consulted Mr Hill, who since the death of Austin took charge of my finances. He was understanding, but he could not advise me on which path to follow – I cannot imagine the poor fellow could have understood the depths and complexities of the matter – and he asked me to do nothing without his consideration. I gave him my word.

Finally, two years ago, in February 1896, Mabel came for a "social visit" accompanied by a Northampton lawyer. In one hand she held a scroll of paper, and for half an hour spoke only of Emily's book. I, feeling myself backed into a corner, clumsily spoke of nothing in particular, while the lawyer, a Mr Spaulding, observed the pair of us as if we were mad.

That night I signed the deed of transfer of land without even reading the paper, hastened by my desire for them to take it, and themselves, away; as if the fact of not seeing it could deny its existence, and I prayed to God that I should die before news of this was made public.

But God did not hear my prayer, and in April the accursed transaction was officially gazetted. And by that time the new and final book of poems of Emily Dickinson was published.

12

J'Accuse

I

This morning Ned appeared charging along the path of the Evergreens, livid with excitement, shouting "Vinnie! Vinnie!" at the top of his voice, as always, with some surprise beneath his cape. I was in the garden, removing the snow from the flower beds with my small and useless spade that everyone has always laughed at. I scarcely heard him, but Maggie came out from the kitchen into the yard to see what the fuss was about. Ned was highly agitated, too much so for his condition, I thought, and I was about to calm him down when he arrived at my side, took me by the arm, and led me towards the house, spade and all. Once in the kitchen he halted to regain his breath while opening a newspaper on the table, pointing at a precise spot. It was the French newspaper *L'Aurore* of 13th January 1898, a month out of date.

"Dreyfus!" gasped the poor lad, exhausted, like the news, while Maggie quickly offered to bring us a pot of tea.

"Good Lord, what has happened now? Has he died?" I asked, horrified and expecting the worst.

"No, but the Court Martial has finally dismissed Esterhazy, and Monsieur Zola published this article that has earned him exile in England. Read it."

Ned had circled in bold ink the title '*J'Accuse*', and at
the bottom of the columns, tight as if written by anger
alone, the signature of Émile Zola. Ned sipped his tea
looking expectantly at me and asking me if I understood
everything, whilst I tried to ignore his insistent questions
and concentrate on my own indignation that was burning
inside. Such disgrace, such humiliation and such injustice!

"Monsieur Zola says that he will not rest until the case
is reopened, that he will not stop even if it means that he
himself also has to go to The Devil's Isle!"

Three years before this, when the Dreyfus *affaire* began to
appear constantly in the international press, and certain
European newspapers were made more available, Ned and
I started following the news with growing interest, our
sympathy unquestionably on the side of Captain Alfred
Dreyfus, and our antipathy, obviously, towards the French
and this unjust court case that was under way.

There is no landscape since Austin died; and since then,
Ned has been my eyes – the eyes that see the world in its
intricate conflicts, the eyes that observe this small community
in its strengths and its miserable weaknesses. Thanks to
Ned, my darling nephew Ned, I've been kept abreast of the
news, and the two of us, through some mysterious reason
– no doubt inherited – adore the criminal trials. And yet we
are both, likewise, infuriated by the injustice of this world.
He has taken the place that Austin would take when Emily
was still with us, a type of guardian, silent protector, less
pompous and far more discreet than his father. Without
doubt more discreet.

These years without Austin have been hard, too hard,
despite everything that happened. Ned knows this too,
and both he and Mattie come to fetch me on Sundays to

have lunch at the Evergreens, with Sue and some such distinguished friend who usually visits for the weekend. I tend to give Maggie the afternoon off, on the condition that she returns by nightfall. At times I am so afraid that Maggie will not return that I make her swear on her ancestors, on the cross, on Jesus, the Holy Gospels and the Pope in Rome, and should anyone else come to mind I'd readily add him to the list. The house at night makes me afraid. Since Emily left us, since Austin abandoned us, this house seems as fragile as a doll's house. I imagine that storms, thieves, ghosts, even huge mice, might come in the night. Every little creak or whisper keeps me awake for hours, planning the quickest route to the kitchen to grab a knife, trying to remember where in the great dark basement I've stored Father's old axe. Less than a hundred yards separate me from the Evergreens, and I like thinking that they would hear me if I shouted loudly, especially given the silence of this valley. But even so I cannot bear the idea of being alone here at night.

There was only one occasion that Maggie was unable to be here on time. I couldn't bring myself to shout for Ned or Mattie and I had no courage to venture along the path in the darkness. As a result I stayed in the kitchen until the small hours, doing God knows how many useless little tasks until finally, overcome by tiredness, I went upstairs to my bedroom. I lay on my bed fully clothed, crossed my arms and said to myself: Vinnie – now let's wait for the thieves. And I fell asleep.

That night I had a nightmare in which Joseph Lyman was standing in the centre of a vast square that I could not recognize, but which seemed to resemble the town square of Amherst. All around him were crowds of people hidden beneath capes of dark cloth, their hoods up, their heads lost in the shadows. It was raining and through the rain you couldn't make anything out. Then one member of the dark crowd, clearly dressed as a soldier, approached Joseph, also in his military uniform, and proceeded to strip him of his decorations, his honours, and even the buttons of his jacket, slicing them off with a small sabre. He then removed Joseph's sword which he proceeded to break by slapping it against his tense leg. The unintelligible, thick mumblings of the crowd now, at the spectacle of the broken sword, turned to shouts, ever more loud and passionate: "Traitor! Traitor!" like in the demotion ceremony of Dreyfus, only that I was also present, beneath one of those dark capes, and I was shouting with the rest, all of us shouting together, while Joseph, on his knees amidst scattered buttons like withered flowers, begged forgiveness.

I awoke at dawn and was unable to sleep again. When Mattie came to find me and to bring me a slice of pie that Sue had made the day before, I told her vaguely that Maggie hadn't returned and that I hadn't found the strength to walk along the path in the snow. Mattie was terribly upset and made me promise that the next time I wouldn't wait till night-time to call her. Since then I repeatedly make Maggie swear, on pain of dreadful punishments at the future hand of my ghost, that she will return home before nightfall.

The question is that now, with that infernal apparatus that Mr Bell is determined to install, almost by force, in every house, everyone believes that they can solve any problem with a shout and the ring of a bell. But what do they hear? What sort of foolishness is this idea of talking through a wire? Austin was of course one of the first to ask the Western for one, and if I weathered his attempts to convince me to have such an apparatus stuck to the wall, it was only because he was my brother; had he not been, I would have given him my full and considered opinion. At the Evergreens they are happy with their latest version of the telephone, especially Ned, whose fixation on it I have to bear instead of Austin's, seeing as he has decided to exchange the object clamped to the wall of the hall with something equally nauseating, but which at least fits on the desk. This machine could help me in an emergency, they tell me, but *that* to me is as if I had suddenly moved miles from here, to Belchertown or Northampton. I tell them that we are only a few yards from each other, that we have *always* been a mere few yards from each other, that a shout from me would be more than enough, and that in any respect Maggie is still somewhat quick and effective in the art of running. So why the bother?

This apparatus has created emergencies. That's what I believe.

In any respect I have rejected the offer, telling them not to waste their time thinking about it, as I wouldn't spoil even an inch of this house with one of those machines, that as far as I'm concerned they could make me ivory dials and earpieces and nothing would change – my health is not going to improve. Quite the opposite; if I have to put up with something so horrible living with me within these four walls, I would sicken rapidly. Everyone has their reasons, no matter how foolish they may seem. Austin used to say that "If anyone puts a stone over me when I am dead, I will get up and go elsewhere!" Fine, well I will never allow a telephone in here, no matter how elegant, sophisticated or useful it may be.

II

Beyond details of the Dreyfus affair, Ned often brings me certain books that he can only get hold of through contacts in the big bookstores of Boston and New York.

Something I find terribly sad is that Emilie is not here with me to share these new discoveries. Amongst them, my favourite is a young aristocratic Englishman named Rudyard Kipling who lives in and writes about India. He has either published little or what reaches me is little, but I'm inclined to believe the former.

At times I believe that Emily would have enjoyed the recognition that she now has, some happiness beyond the praise of a couple of poems in the local newspaper or in compilations thanks to the solidarity of Helen Jackson. How many people would have known how to appreciate my sister when she was still alive? Now, with the poems published, and in various editions, it seems an absurd question. Everyone is certain that she was a sort of genius recluse and, even worse, everyone claims to have known this for ever. Blasted hypocrites, none of this is certain.

A while ago, in a rather delicate conversation concerning my proceedings with Mabel, Sue confessed to me that a few months after Emily's death she had selected various poems out of those that Emily had dedicated to her and had sent them to Colonel Higginson, stating clearly her intention to publish them, but asking his advice at the same time. This was, according to her, before the time that I had asked her to make a selection of the thousands of poems that I had found in Emilie's secretaire after the funeral.

Higginson received the poems from Sue, and, to her great surprise, replied promptly. They were imperfect, he said. They were still showing the imperfections of rhyme, and although they were not lacking in the accustomed genius and energy, they were ambiguous, too cryptic, indecipherable for most readers. No, was the Colonel's verdict, these poems were not ready to be published, they were not before, and perhaps they never would be. They were, according to the words he let slip one night that he was in Amherst in November of that same year, "unpresentable". He said, moreover, that it would be a grave error to send them anywhere, although, according to Sue, he brazenly suggested that she herself put together, through her own resources, a home-made edition for friends and neighbours. Sue, however, considered this an insult to Emily, something that Emily could have done at any stage during her life had she wanted to. If Higginson were so sure that those poems were imperfect, better to go with his opinion and keep the material for another occasion. When I later approached Sue with my collection of recently unearthed poems, seeking her help in publishing them, she replied evasively and delayed giving a definite answer for nearly two years. A strange attitude, I would say, incomprehensible in a woman who had known Emily like nobody else had, and who, moreover, understood perfectly the value of the material that she had in her hands. At the time I could not forgive her for this, and it was in essence her negative reaction that prompted me in my anxiety to place my trust in Mabel for the publication of the poems.

Ah – had I known in time! Sue did not want to demoralize me, she did not want to sully the perfect image of Emily, nor place herself nor me in a potential conflict. For Sue, Emily's genius could not be stained, and yet for me, her genius must shine forth come what may.

A short while ago, thanks to Mattie, we found out that another of the poets initially "rejected" by the Colonel, albeit a long time before, is the Brooklyn poet that everyone is now talking about: Mr Walt Whitman. Higginson, what a strange déjà vu, alleged that they were a handful of "imperfect poems". But Whitman paid no heed to the criticism and apparently put all the work that he had – not much one might imagine – in a home-made edition, just as Higginson had suggested as a delicate and useless gesture so as not to dishearten the poet entirely. From the moment the famous book appeared – the first official edition was some years ago, we're now at the ninth – nobody talks of anything else in New York. That handful of imperfect poems shines on the bookshelves of every bookstore in America. What's more, it's even been said that anyone who wants to know this country need do no more than read *Leaves of Grass*.

What was it that drove Colonel Higginson to accept my proposition to be the principal editor of my sister's work after rejecting Sue's offer in such a negative and hurtful fashion? I know that some people have suggested that it was my eloquence at reciting, and even *I* have believed that in moments of vanity. But let's not be fooled. I must confess that the only explanation for this sudden change of opinion of the value of the poems had nothing to do with my eloquence nor with my obstinacy, but something far simpler than this: Higginson never in reality changed his opinion.

I can see it now, and I suppose I knew it when I read the letter that he sent me following the publication of the first volume, brief lines that reflected his unconcealable surprise at the success of the book in Boston and at the astuteness of the critics in certain well-known journals. This is the pure, sad truth: he believed that he had released merely a little hummingbird, fragile and ephemeral, and yet what he now had was a falcon whose wings overshadowed him. He was surely banking on the elegant rejection of two or three editors, and yet suddenly, with Mabel's assistance, her hunger for recognition and her natural speed at making any corrections that occurred to her, he cannot have wasted any time. Herein lies the mystery, this sudden illumination of the Colonel that Sue cannot understand.

If there had been any clarification, it took place after his generous help, not while the voice of Emilie dwelt among those small bits of paper with violet pencil, but much later, when her voice appeared from the review columns of the journals and newspapers.

III

The time of waiting is driving me mad.

Winter is intolerable, the harsh cold that whistles through every crack, the snow that never ceases to fall, as if God Himself wished to bury the valley in a white shroud and rid Himself of our sins. Or just my sins. Perhaps He only wishes to forget me and my worries, and to bury me in this maddening silence.

God is right in doing so. I do not deserve His compassion.

It has been nearly two years since I sued Mabel for fraud.

It was May 1896 and it had then been ten years since Emily's death. I went to take flowers to the cemetery, needing some peace to think, to find some way out of a situation that seemed to me irredeemable. The good natured symmetry of cemeteries, with the regular patches of green grass and mute and invariable faces of stone, is for me, and always has been, a refuge for the spirit. I remember that I felt so exasperated by the events that it was a great effort even to walk out of the house. I felt that I had finally reached the end of my strength, that I could no longer carry other people's burdens on my tired shoulders. There, in the cemetery, I decided that I had by now fulfilled my duty with respect to Emily, and that *now* was the time to make good the errors.

Although Austin may have turned in his grave, Mabel Todd was not going to have her way if I could possibly prevent it.

The notice of land transfer had spread rapidly since it was officially gazetted. Mr Hill, when he found out, resolutely concluded that I had betrayed his advice and counsel, and he resigned at once from dealing with my finances. To my regret, I now recognize that he was right.

Sue, from the coast of Maine, made her feelings about the events in Amherst known to me in a note addressed to me but written by Ned, in a threatening and harsh tone wholly unlike her.

"I trust, for the good of the family, that they are no more than unfounded rumours," she concluded.

Mabel and her husband had, fortunately, left for Japan for six months, but not without first making effective and public the transfer of that blessed plot of land. Everything was now public, and it appeared to everyone's eyes precisely what it was in reality: an inexplicable gift. Only *I* knew why I had acted in that way, but that was not going to help me climb out of the hole in which I found myself. Prove that it had been an extortion? Blackmail? The publication of that book lacked sufficient value for anyone besides myself, and yet on the other hand she could quite easily claim that she had been working on details of the book that I was not aware of, which would account for the delay in providing the finished manuscript.

No, with the truth I was not going to get anywhere. I therefore opted for the only possible alternative: to lie. I accused Mabel Todd of having secured my signature on that deed of transfer through deception, making me believe that the document concerned some other matter. It was true that there had been a direct witness, that Spaulding fellow, well fine, I would deny it. Step by step I would deny all that he had seen me forced to do in complying with the dying wishes of my brother and the greedy wishes of that bloodsucker. I would deny it to whoever I deemed it necessary, I would commit perjury and would burn in hell because of it, but before dying I would settle both my account, and that of the Dickinsons.

And that it was I resolved to do, two years ago now.

When Sue returned from Maine we had a lengthy conversation in which she confessed to me her true opinion about Higginson with respect to the publication of Emily's poems. We spoke openly, as we had not done for so long, about Austin, Emily and Gilbert – about Mabel. She also promised me that she would stand by me in anything; she, Ned and Mattie would support me like the mast of the boat of Ulysses, until the storm passed and the slippery songs of the Sirens were a mere memory.

Since then, even in the midst of this nerve-racking wait, there is a certain level of peace in my soul. I know what I have to do, and I know why and for whom.

The court hearing has been scheduled for the first of March. However, Maggie has been called to make a testimony that will be read out later as a deposition, because she has announced that she will not be in Massachusetts at that date. Scarcely had she returned than I asked her what she had said. "The truth, Miss Vinnie. No more no less than the truth," she replied. Hammond, the lawyer, who was present during the testimony, said that she was devastating, that Maggie held nothing back about the secret liaisons between Mabel and Austin both in my house and in the Evergreens, about the shameless frequency of their walks and their orders to her to prepare them a picnic lunch to eat in the woods. She spoke of the hours the two of them would spend locked in the library, and of the gifts that Austin would give her, in such a way that if this testimony were to reach the public, it would cause a tremendous scandal.

I explained to Hammond that I had no desire whatsoever for that testimony to be read in court, that if it came to that I would rather lose the case altogether. I cannot destroy the little recollection that is left of my brother's dignity in such a vulgar and petty manner. Hammond told me not to worry, that the person least likely of all to want such information spread around would be Mabel, as for her it would condemn her for life on moral grounds alone. He said, smiling, and according to him paraphrasing Tacitus, *"divulgata atque incredibilia avide accepta sunt."*

I think the lawyer is a morbid man at heart...

13

Tell All the Truth but Tell It Slant

Tell all the Truth but tell it slant –
Success in Circuit lies –
Too bright for our infirm Delight
The Truth's superb surprise.

As Lightning to the Children eased
With explanation kind
The Truth must dazzle gradually
Or every man be blind.

– E. Dickinson

I

*T*his morning, to my surprise and fear, the courtroom was heaving with people.

The majority of those who were there, with their mouths twisted into grim and expectant smiles, were family relations of some sort, some of them indeed quite close family, but in my nervous state they all seemed strangers; and if I did manage to recall a name or two, I could not feel anything in my heart.

Judge Hopkins, tall, dressed in solemn black like a poplar tree in mourning, waited for the performers of the spectacle – that's to say me and the Todds. Mattie had run on ahead to find a seat but Ned walked by my side, holding me firmly by the arm, dear fellow, so firmly that as we entered the courtroom I thought I should cry out with pain. I also felt a strong urge to shake him off and ask him, please, to leave me alone – alone as I had been all these years, alone with myself, alone with the exhausting ghost of my sister, alone with Maggie. She knew all of this and yet would never be able to help because she was with me like only the Irish can be, impassive, hard like a stone, and useless for the soul. Maggie was my solemn support, she always has been and surely always will be for us; but my heart remained unprotected, even though I might be with her twenty-four hours a day.

Yes, I did want to ask Ned to leave. I also felt that I would bear everything that was to come better if it weren't for Sue, who doubtless at that moment was shut away in her house, licking her open, festering wounds of bitterness, compelled not to leave the house by her pride, affectation, malice, pain – whatever it was – I understood. How could I not understand? But the result was that she was not at my side, not even *on* my side, but rather on the side of the ill-begotten revenge that was eating away at her. Oh to be alone. Alone! Far from Austin's ghost, so irresponsible; far from fastidious Mattie, so comprehensible; far from Sue's hatred, so ghastly; far from Father's ghost, so omnipresent; and far from Mother's ghost, as familiar as my own skirt.

And yet Ned, my darling Ned, remained calm at my side, holding me with an unaccustomed force as if he feared that I was going to fall. His presence, firm yet so close to my heart, was a soothing balm that I could not do without, not even when my spirit rebelled against all the issues that kept falling upon my shoulders.

There we were, in the Northampton Superior Court, a place that even in my worst dreams I'd never imagined entering such as I was at that moment, bound to my nephew like a tiny black limb, with all the grim looks of everyone, including the Judge, upon me – good Judge Hopkins, who had respected Father so much, fervent Republicans the pair of them, dry and austere like two marble sculptures.

In a certain sense – in more than one sense – it was I who was being judged, by my own Father.

There was Mrs Clark in the front row, with her ridiculous bonnet and her bird-like features pecking at the crumbs of the world. And there was Mr Clark on her left, doubtless bored to death by his own wife. And there the

Roshline sisters, sitting straight-backed behind the Clarks, symmetrical in their dresses and weepy faces. How could I ask these people to leave? How could I ask anyone? How could I explain to them how much I loathed this whole affair?

Beyond, at the other end of the court, I saw Mabel. David was reading a journal as if nothing bothered him too much. Cretin. In any respect he had always been like that, at least one honest spirit amongst so much vulgarity. Mabel was not reading, she didn't even appear to be aware of anything around her. She was sitting in the centre of a bench, alone, very upright, with an aura of supreme disdain, or an indestructible faith in herself. However I did realize that she also appeared suddenly quite aged, quite worn down, despite her efforts to disguise it. I myself now had nothing to lose. But she? What would become of her long conferences about Emily Dickinson when all this was over?

I cursed her without mercy, without a shred of Christian compassion, as free of doubt as I was of regret. The question is: how could I have ever loved her? How could I, Emily, Mother, and even Sue have esteemed her so much at the beginning? How could we not have known who Mabel really was?

Ah – how I detested her now! How I loathed this *gift to the world*!

What's more, the shameless wretch was still wearing the ring that Austin gave her; and as a token of mourning she wore a veil of black crape over her bonnet. My hands tingled with the violent urge to charge over there and tear off this veil, to tear off her hat, her hair, her head, and to scream at her, there, in front of everyone, that Austin had died three years ago because of her, that perhaps, and only perhaps, he had been happy at her and her husband's side, or with

her husband's consent, happily acting out the role of the
faded and powerful lover, but that this happiness was of no
interest to anyone, that no one could be concerned with a
happiness that engendered so much pain and humiliation.
Did they want to be happy? Happy – well, they could have
left together for Nevada, Mexico, hell, for all I care. And
yet to have gone to hell they would have needed to go no
further than Amherst, which was where all the rest of us
were, thanks to her wretched happiness.

You see they didn't leave, although I know that they
thought about it and that Austin's trip to Texas was not
coincidental, but they never left. They remained in order
to be "happy" at our side – Emilie, with her vision fixed on
the strange world of her room, buried in her own affairs to
such a degree that her beloved Sue would inevitably end
up hating her – I, looking everywhere so as not to see, or at
least that's what I now believe after so much time – all of
us secretly knowing the truth and yet in our hearts never
wanting to accept it until its irrefutability forced us to.
Afterwards, Emilie had died, Gilbert had died, and it was
as if my brother wanted to bury himself within himself and
disregard everything and everyone that wasn't related to
his obsession. Austin had changed overnight into the most
selfish of all beings. I have no idea if he was waiting for
Emilie to die, or whether it was her death that unleashed
such misery in him.

For he was a good man, my brother. He was a good man.

It is for that reason, or better to say for his small remaining
honour, that nothing about his relationship with Mabel
can be revealed, at least not inside this den of thieves and
liars. And it is also for that reason, amongst others, that
I, the Dickinson zealot, was standing there alone in that
courtroom. Alone.

"Shhh," whispered Ned.

"What?" I asked, startled.

I had lost all notion of time and space. This was something that was starting to happen to me quite often, simply through being old, I imagined, although I would never admit as much to anyone, least of all Ned, who adored me.

"What happened?" I asked him again quietly.

"You were talking to yourself, that's what happened."

"Merciful God... Did you hear anything?"

"Papa's name."

"Anything else?"

"Yes. And please – people are going to think that we've hidden away another old madwoman," he said seriously, although I knew that the sly fox was actually holding back his laughter.

"Insolent boy, a little respect please! Your aunt Emily was no old woman. And for your information she had not one grey hair."

"That's because she dyed her hair red...'

The mere idea of Emilie dyeing her hair was so outrageous that we both burst out laughing as if we'd been in the garden at home. Oh – how I would have loved to have been in my garden at that moment, with Ned, making jokes about the family while we transplanted the first bulbs for summer.

But no. We were at the Northampton Superior Court, in the main courtroom itself, a place far removed from any garden, opaque and solemn, like that leaden day of that frozen month of March. Of the sixty-five Marches that had passed through my life, this one was the worst of them all.

Judge Hopkins rose to his feet and cleared his throat to bring the court to order.

"The show's about to begin..." whispered Ned at my side.

And that's what it was.

II

"...We are gathered here in the Superior Court of the city of Northampton on the first day of March of the year 1898, to determine the case of Dickinson v. Todd. In the presentation of the same the following is stated: that the plaintiff, Miss Lavinia Norcross Dickinson, of Amherst, did sign the deed by which she transferred part of her property to the beneficiary here present, the defendant Mrs Mabel Loomis Todd, also of Amherst; that this act was performed without the knowledge *ipso facto* that said document was in fact a legal deed and conveyance of real estate, and that it represented a forfeiture of all rights to that land; that, on the contrary, the beneficiary secured the signature of the donor on a deed that the donor understood to be a written agreement that inhibited the construction of buildings upon the plot of land in question. Acting on behalf of Dickinson is the firm Hammond & Field, represented by Mr Hammond and Mr Taft, and on behalf of Loomis Todd, the firm Hamlin & Reilly, represented by Mr Hamlin and Mr O'Donnell. I accordingly open the first session. As was stipulated yesterday, Mr Hammond will present his case first."

William Hammond rose ceremoniously from his chair and thanked the Judge with a short bow. He then moved to the front of the court, raised his arms like a martyr exhausted by pitching his complaints to the Heavens in his fight for eternal justice, and, in bolder advocacy than that of Judge Hopkins, he gladly opened the case with a single question, marvellously theatrical:

"How does one differentiate between a transfer and a fraudulent seizure?"

A stunned silence spread across the courtroom, followed moments later by murmurs of appreciation for Hammond, who remained immobile, his back to the Judge, staring furiously at us as if divine grace had suddenly possessed him, and no longer was he a mere mortal lawyer but an archangel of Justice sent to earth by a spirit greater than he. Hammond was well-known as much for appearing to enjoy the histrionic side of his job as for the excellence of his submissions and speeches.

"The answer is simple," he continued. "Free will, ladies and gentlemen, the free will of the donor to cede to the other party. The history of generosity of the Dickinson family could very well give an account of a gift. But it was this very generosity, however, that allowed the mockery of what is commonly called "good faith". Or, in clearer language: fraud. Lavinia Norcross Dickinson is the only remaining descendant of one of the most distinguished families of this area, one of the families whose participation in the social and cultural life of this valley has been profound. Her father, Edward Dickinson, was the most respected neighbour and lawyer of Amherst, and, I dare to add, of this city of Northampton; as was her brother, William Austin Dickinson, dearly missed since he passed away three years ago. Her sister, Emily Dickinson, has been and doubtlessly will continue to be considered one of this country's best poets, immortalized already in the recently appeared volumes of poetry, known to all of you here.

"For her part, Mrs Mabel Loomis Todd and Professor Todd, prominent neighbours of Amherst, own a house a few yards from the Dickinson Homestead. Between both properties is to be found a small plot of forested land without buildings. Mrs Todd, on several occasions, requested Miss Dickinson for a written agreement to prohibit the construction of any new buildings upon this sector of the property. Miss Dickinson, agreeing without hesitation to said request, did not consider the agreement to be effective until 1896 when, taking advantage of a formal visit, Mrs Todd secured the signature of Miss Dickinson upon a legal deed, that in effect was not a restrictive covenant, but a forfeiture of said property, which accordingly passed into the ownership of Mr and Mrs Todd. After the death of William Austin Dickinson, Lavinia Dickinson granted Mr Lawrence Hill, neighbour of the community, notary and personal friend of my client, the financial control of the family estate. Subsequently, the transfer of land took place, signed by Lavinia Dickinson alone, without Mr Hill's knowledge, and with the collusion, possibly unaware of the circumstances, of a single witness, Mr Theodore Spaulding, of Northampton.

"These, in essence, are the facts, Your Honour."

"Let us move then to direct questioning," said Judge Hopkins matter-of-factly, uncomfortable with the extent of the presentation. "Miss Dickinson, be so kind as to approach the witness box and be seated."

III

HAMMOND-DICKINSON

"Lavinia Norcross Dickinson, do you swear to tell the truth, the whole truth and nothing but the truth?"

"Yes, I swear." (*Please God, I beg you not to abandon me now!*)

"Good, we'll begin. Miss Dickinson, are you the owner of the plot of land currently in dispute?" Hammond asked, pointing to a rectangle drawn with thick crayon upon a plan of the valley mounted on a board.

I looked at him feigning studious contemplation; I know better than anyone every detail of my inheritance, but I know especially well that terrible, accursed strip of land.

"Yes."

"Could you tell us how you came by this property?"

"Before her death, my sister Emily Dickinson left all her estate to my name. Following the death of my brother, William Austin Dickinson, all the family estate likewise went into my hands through the expressed wish of his will, owing to the fact that I am the only direct surviving descendant of my father, Edward Dickinson."

"Herewith legal copies of both wills," said Hammond. "How long have you known Mrs Mabel Todd and her husband, Professor David Todd?"

"Approximately fourteen years."

"They acquired the land bordering, or practically bordering, the Dickinson house."

"That is correct."

"And Mrs Todd demanded that no buildings of any sort were to be raised on the plot that borders their property."

"She did not demand it, but she did request on repeated occasions a written agreement from me not to allow any construction there."

"And you accepted?"

"Not immediately. I left it abundantly clear that my word was sufficient."

"However, your word appears not to have been sufficient for Mrs Todd."

"I suppose not." (*Nothing is sufficient for Mrs Todd, Mr Hammond.*)

"What exactly happened when Mrs Todd, in the company of Mr Spaulding, visited you the afternoon of 7th February 1896? Had they made clear the purpose of their visit prior to arriving?"

"No. I imagined it to be another social visit."

"Did you know the lawyer Theodore Spaulding?"

"Not personally."

"Could you tell us what happened during the visit?"

"We spoke at length about Emily's book. Mrs Todd, at my behest I must add, had taken charge of the transcription of my sister's most relevant poems for the edition. We spoke at length about the work she had recently been performing on the edition, the third volume of poems, if I remember correctly."

"And the payment or recompense for this work?"

"No, we did not speak of this. Until quite recently I had understood that Mrs Todd would do this work without a fee, 'a labour of love' in her own words, and that the immense literary repercussion and economic earnings obtained through this work would be a more than sufficient reward."

"Let us return to the visit. What happened next?"

"In the preceding days we had also spoken about the written agreement of not building upon the bordering plot. I insisted on a verbal agreement – it was a question of honour, if you like – but she proved extremely anxious about the topic, so finally I agreed to put my word in writing. Before leaving, Mrs Todd showed me a paper, a document of regular size and appearance, and she asked me to sign it, as we had agreed."

"Mr Spaulding said nothing?"

"He asked me if I wished to read it. I answered that I knew what it was about, that there was no need to dwell on the matter, and I signed."

"What happened after signing?"

"Nothing. I said goodbye to them at the front door of my house, just as I say goodbye to all my guests. The following day Mrs Todd embarked for Japan with her husband."

"When did you find out that in reality you had ceded ownership of the land in question?"

"In the month of May, 1896, when notice of the transfer was officially gazetted."

"Did you know, or suspect for one minute, the nature of the document that you had signed?"

"No." (*Forgive me, Lord. Forgive me.*)

"Did you notice any stamp, or any indication that it was a legal deed?"

"No."

"Are you sure?"

"Absolutely."

"Nothing more for the moment," said Hammond.

Judge Hopkins then ordered a recess until midday.

We went to have lunch with Ned at the house of the Clarks. Ned spoke animatedly with Mrs Clark, while Mr Clark and I remained silent, praying that they wouldn't include us in the conversation. I could scarcely touch my food. I wanted to lie down for a bit, but I could never rest in other people's houses, and returning to Amherst was impossible.

Immediately after the recess Mr Dwight Palmer, property agent of Amherst, was called to testify. Mr Hammond attacked first.

"My question, Mr Palmer, is specific. How much would you estimate, according to the market of the area, the value of the piece of land currently disputed?"

While he spoke, Hammond had gone up to the board with the map of the Dickinson property and was pointing once again with his stick to the rectangle. Palmer did not even look.

"Between six hundred and six hundred and fifty dollars."

"That is all," Hammond said.

Hamlin, the defence, indifferent, decided that the witness was of no interest and continued noting things on his papers.

Seeing that Palmer remained in the witness box as if awaiting more questions, Judge Hopkins indicated to him that he could step down.

Palmer blinked in surprise and returned to his seat. His role in the most famous hearing of the year was over.

IV

HAMLIN-TODD

Mr Hamlin opened the defence. He was a gaunt man, of dark complexion and dry features, noticeably lacking the arrogance and theatricalities of Mr Hammond, but with that characteristic sharpness of one who pays close attention to the gestures of others, to those imperceptible hesitations and revealing evasive remarks of insecurity or falsehood. With his frankly indifferent gestures he was almost as intimidating as Hammond, and it was quite clear to everyone that he deplored the theatrical performances of his adversary.

"This defence," he began, "does not object to nor call into question the fact that Miss Lavinia Dickinson signed the deed of transfer, and that the signature corresponds to hers. Nor does the defence presuppose that Miss Dickinson lacks, or lacked at the time, any intellectual faculty. However, and considering what Mr Hammond made dramatically clear in his presentation, it appears strange that a woman such as Miss Dickinson, accustomed to taking charge of the family affairs, should allege that she was unaware of the nature of the legal deed that she was signing, as far as not even taking the effort to read it. In any respect, let us suppose for a moment that this be the truth, it still is not the nucleus of the problem. What is of concern is precisely that which thus far has been carefully avoided: a natural promise of payment for qualified services. My client, Mrs Mabel Loomis Todd, carried out the literary task mentioned over a period of several years, without receiving recompense beyond this 'promise of pay', firstly from Mr William Austin Dickinson, and later, when said gentleman was deceased, from his sister, Miss Lavinia Dickinson, of Amherst. Given these circumstances..."

But Hamlin was prevented from continuing by the interruption of Judge Hopkins.

"Do you accordingly wish to base your defence on the fact that the release of land had been previously agreed upon in consideration for the literary work carried out by Mrs Todd?"

"In effect, yes."

"This is not stated in writing, Mr Hamlin..."

"It is what this defence has considered at the moment... given the circumstances."

The hitherto impassive expression of Judge Hopkins here revealed a flash of irritation.

"Proceed," he said, and allowed Hamlin to continue with the presentation of his case.

"Permit me to establish the nature of the work in question. Mrs Mabel Loomis Todd, would you come to the witness box?"

Mabel Todd rose from her place with the haughtiness and displeasure of one who is doing someone else a terrific favour, and walked up to the box without deigning to look at anyone. *Still with that accursed custom of painting on her dress exotic birds, oriental flowers, whatever extravagant object that separates her from the common horde, that shows to the unknowing world her multiple talents.* Mr Hamlin made her swear the accustomed oath.

"Mrs Todd, could you tell us when and for what motives you began to work in connection with the Dickinson family?"

"My work began approximately in the year 1888, when I came into contact for the first time with the work of Emily Dickinson. It continued until a couple of years ago – 1896 I would say. Until the death of Mr Dickinson. Miss Lavinia asked me especially, she begged me, to undertake the work. She wished at all costs to publish the poems of her sister Emily."

"It was she who gave you the originals upon which you were to work?"

"Yes. In August 1888 Miss Lavinia came to see me with a box full of papers, some sewn into fascicles, others, the majority, loose. There were around one thousand poems written by the hand of Emily Dickinson. Apparently, Colonel Thomas W. Higginson had promised to help with the publication and to look for an editor for the work of Emily, but he needed the material organized, classified and polished. This was the work that she asked me to perform."

"And could you describe the exact nature of the work?"

"Editing. Selecting, editing and copying those poems on my typewriter. The second part, selecting and polishing the poems, I performed in collaboration with Colonel Higginson, principal editor of the volumes that have so far appeared published."

"Editing, selecting and copying. Would you say that this was a difficult task? In other words, could any one of us here present have undertaken it?"

"My work was utterly specialized. By no means could anyone do it. It requires experience, studiousness, patience, intuition, aesthetic sensitivity, and above all, a profound knowledge of poetry. I am convinced that these are not qualities widely held these days."

"And you possess such qualities?"

"Naturally. If not I would have been unable to accept even touching the work of someone like Miss Emily. And had I not possessed these qualities, neither would Miss Lavinia, I am certain, have entrusted me with so... sensitive and delicate a task."

"And so you spent ten years working upon this?"

"Intermittently, yes. Ten years. But please bear in mind that I was absent from Amherst for prolonged periods. My husband is obliged to travel almost permanently, and I accompany him."

"For a work of such quantity and quality of effort, had you previously agreed to any type of payment?"

Mabel hesitated.

"In a certain sense, yes."

"What manner of payment, Mrs Todd?"

"Mr Dickinson promised that he would cede to me the strip of land that borders his property and ours."

"You are referring to the land in question?"

"Precisely. When Austin died, he entrusted Lavinia with the fulfilment of this promise. We spoke about the matter on various occasions."

"And why, in that case, did Mr Dickinson himself not carry out the promise? If he was aware of the effort of your work, why did he himself not sign the release with his own signature, while he still lived?"

"I suppose that... so as not to create conflicts. Our families had grown apart. On the other hand he would have done it, without doubt, but death took him by surprise before he was able to. We were all taken by surprise with his death."

Mabel cleared her throat, as if trying to quell an emotion that she was not prepared to show in public.

"I am led to understand," said Hamlin, "that the person authorized to fulfil the release of the land in question was his sister Lavinia, Miss Dickinson."

"That is correct."

There ensued a long silence, during which Mr Hamlin appeared to have run out of words. Finally, with a dispassionate tone he asked:

"Mrs Todd, would you consider that you obtained the signature of Miss Dickinson through improper means?"

"Absolutely not. All I did was to ask her to sign that which her brother had promised."

"Thank you. That is all," said Hamlin.

Judge Hopkins chose not to interrupt the session with another recess, and called Hamlin to continue with his cross-examination.

V

HAMLIN-DICKINSON

"Miss Dickinson, what exactly was the arrangement that you made with Mrs Todd with respect to the poems of your sister, Emily Dickinson?"

"I asked her to select and copy, in a clear and legible hand, the poems that according to her assessment were the most appropriate – the best."

"Only to select and copy?"

"Only to select and copy."

"And did Mrs Todd appear to be flattered by the request? Shall we say, enthusiastic?"

"It was necessary to ask her several times, if that answers your question."

"But finally she agreed to do it. Did you come to an agreement about the payment of said work?"

"I did not offer it as work. I asked her as a personal favour, and because while Emily was alive she had insisted on knowing her. Given the admiration that she demonstrated towards my sister, and given the close relationship that she maintained with my family, it occurred to me that she would be the most appropriate person to ask of such a favour. Evidently it was not to be so."

"Referring to what? Did she turn out to be unsuitable for the work?"

"Nobody, especially not I, could deny her suitability for such artistic endeavours. What I meant is that Mrs Todd's criteria were too... self-sufficient."

"And you would consider this a negative attribute?"

"Inconvenient, I would say."

"Miss Dickinson, are you satisfied with the publication of the poems of your sister, Emily Dickinson?"

"Of course, it was my decision. I do not even know if my sister would have agreed to it, but I deemed that the world had more right to her work than the inside of a chest of drawers. Or the fire."

"I understand. Do you agree, therefore, with the form in which the poems are edited, the compilation, the corrections, the appearance of the book, the work of Mr Higginson?"

"I have no objection to the work of Colonel Higginson. As for the rest, the fact that my sister's work has appeared to the world is more important for me than any other aesthetic consideration."

"Miss Dickinson, I'll put it in another way: are you satisfied with the work that my client, Mrs Mabel Todd, carried out on the works of your sister Emily Dickinson?"

"I have no objections to the work of Mrs Todd."

"And would you consider this work to deserve some remuneration?"

No – of course not! That leech deserves nothing. She didn't deserve to have Sue open her doors to her, nor that my nephew fell in love with her, nor that my brother dedicated a single moment of his life to her!

"Miss Dickinson, would you consider this work to deserve some remuneration?"

"The... the personal fame that Mrs Todd has acquired
thanks to this work, the economic return she receives from the
conferences about my sister and from the articles published
about my sister. Does all this seem a modest remuneration?"

"But I am referring to a strictly economic payment."

"And I am taking about real payment, Mr Hamlin."

*Her name on the cover of Emilie's book, Mabel Todd, for
Heaven's sake! Who the hell is Mabel Todd to be there, alongside
the name of Higginson and Emily herself? Public recognition,
the acknowledgement of falsity that is spoken so often about
in this courtroom, and all that I dare not mention for shame,
Mr Hamlin. All that I keep quiet about to preserve the good
name of my brother, because from David Todd's employment
to the house in which they live – it's all thanks to Austin. And
that corrupt ease with which they move from city to city, from
country to country, talking about what they never knew and
receiving the royalties of that treachery – they owe this not to
Emily Dickinson but to me, Mr Hamlin, to me. It was I who
placed in her hands the only thing of value she has ever touched
– the poems of my sister...*

"Do you feel all right, Miss Dickinson?"

*I am fed up, sickened, Mr Hamlin, sickened to the core of
such misery, knowing that I have a guilty conscience thanks to
that woman, knowing that I will end up in hell thanks to that
woman, thanks to her and her rat of a husband, thanks to the
pair of them, Mr Hamlin, thanks to that pair of bloodsucking
leeches, leeches, leeches...*

"Miss Dickinson?"

"Leeches. That's what they are. No more no less. Leeches!"

Hamlin looked in my direction astonished.

Ned half-rose to his feet, as if unsure whether to approach
the box or sit down again.

The gavel of Judge Hopkins resounded dryly through the silence that suddenly reigned in the courtroom. Before anyone could reconstruct what had happened, he sharply ordered a recess until the following day.

It was a scandal.

In all my life I have no recollection of ever having lost control like that. I didn't feel myself physically indisposed; my hands weren't shaking nor my heart beating in my breast, quite the contrary, but soon after the outburst an almost unnatural feeling of calm and peace came over my soul. This new lightness of spirit, however, prevented me registering any of the voices or images around me, as if everything was happening too quickly, or so slowly that my own mind, unable to be at rest, jumped from one thing to the next. I was conscious of what had just happened in the courtroom, but from then onwards reality acquired that viscous texture of dreams.

Nor can I remember how we returned to Amherst; I only know that Ned was with me and that some strange voice repeated quietly, like a prayer, that it wanted to go home, to go home.

VI

TAFT-TODD

I would like not to have to appear in court ever again.

If it were up to me I would leave matters as they stand. I would abandon everything right here. But I cannot. Hammond said, before coming into the courtroom this morning, that the outlook seems excellent, and that Maggie's deposition is crucial should any other... eventuality, occur. I know that intimately he is convinced that

I am mad, mad in a different way from my sister but mad all the same.

The examination continued with Mr Taft. Mr Hamlin, according to what I was told, decided not to pursue my testimony. The truth of the matter is that yesterday caused more commotion and pity than actual scandal. Without wishing to, it appears, I have managed to tip the balance of opinion in my favour.

"Whatever happens, please, keep calm," the lawyers begged me. "Another outburst could cause more damage than good after yesterday." I agreed, of course. But when I saw *her* enter and sit in the box with that look of hunger that no amount of mourning can disguise... I had to struggle to think of other things while Mabel responded to the questions of Mr Taft.

"Mrs Todd, I am led to believe that you and your husband have lived for several years in a house of the Queen Anne style beyond the property of the Dickinsons, is that not so?"

"That is correct. Dell has been our house since 1887."

"In 1887 you took possession of the house. To whom did it belong prior to this? I am led to believe that the property had already been built, but that it was not yet completed."

"It belonged to Mr William Austin Dickinson. My husband and I acquired it through him."

"Could you tell us the value of the transaction?"

"I know nothing of values. Perhaps my husband remembers."

"With respect to the deed of transfer that Miss Dickinson signed to your name, could you tell us who it was who drew it up?"

"I myself drew up the deed, saving only the words 'considering other values'."

"Do you know to whom the added text belonged?"

"I suppose to Mr Spaulding."

"Mrs Todd, did you speak on any occasion to Miss Dickinson with regard to the payment that you would receive as remuneration from the work of copying that you carried out?"

"Yes, on one occasion we spoke of the matter, and she agreed with me that the work should be rewarded. And it was more than a mere job of copying, as I said before, but of selecting, editing, creating clean copies of over one thousand poems."

"Let us return to the deed of transfer. When did you speak to Mr Spaulding about the matter for the first time?"

"In January of 1896. I had written to him about it and taken the matter to him personally. Before this I had spoken to Miss Dickinson about it. She said that if I had the deed drawn up, she would sign it with pleasure. This is what I communicated to Mr Spaulding, and we arranged his journey to Amherst for the following week, to sign the document. I believe I remember having left the paper with Mr Spaulding and that he sent it back to my house a few days later."

"On the day that you met with Mr Spaulding at the house of Miss Dickinson, do you remember the time of day?"

"Perfectly, as we have already mentioned. It was six o'clock in the evening."

"Could you tell us what happened next?"

"We spoke about Emily's poems, about the latest edition and the plans for the next. Miss Dickinson showed Mr Spaulding the china dinner-set of the family. We took tea at the dining-room table. Finally, after no more than an hour, I told Vinnie that we had brought the document, that it was ready to sign and that Mr Spaulding was fully briefed on the subject."

"What does 'fully briefed' mean?"

"About the transfer, and the fact that Vinnie – Miss Dickinson – had explicitly asked that it not be made official immediately – that it should be a discreet affair, in other words."

"Did you make clear that the document was a legal deed of conveyance?"

"I believe so."

"Did you discuss the written agreement not to allow construction upon the land?"

"I do not recall speaking in particular about construction."

"But neither do you recall speaking in particular about the deed of transfer."

"As I said, I believe I did mention it."

"But you are not sure."

"Sir, it was a subject upon which we had both already reached an agreement, and about which we had spoken on numerous occasions. What I mean is that under those circumstances some details are taken as understood, and there is no need to discuss them so... explicitly."

"Do you remember whether Miss Dickinson made any comment as she read the document?"

"I do not remember her reading it. Nor do I remember any comments with respect to it."

"Do you remember whether Mr Spaulding mentioned that the document was a legal property deed?"

"I believe so, but I cannot be certain."

"This was in the month of January. You asked Mr Spaulding not to publicize the transfer immediately. Is that not so?"

"Well, this was more in consideration for the request that Miss Dickinson had made than from my own volition."

"What happened next?"

"The following day I left with my husband for Japan."

Immediately after Mabel, her husband was called to testify. David Todd went up to the witness box slowly, and aside from a small twitching of his cane against the wooden floor, a rhythmic tapping that was scarcely noticeable, he did not appear worried or nervous. At least his expression denoted no more than natural expectation.

"Mr Todd, could you tell us when, and under what circumstances, you spoke to Miss Dickinson about the transference of this plot of land destined for your wife?"

"Miss Dickinson inspected the land. A visual inspection. It occurred a few days before the meeting that my wife referred to a few minutes ago, in January 1896. It was night, but there was a full moon and she eventually resolved to make the inspection under those conditions. Then she came to our house to tell me that she understood perfectly the limits of the land, and that she was quite prepared to sign the deed whenever we considered it necessary."

"That inspection and the visit to your house took place on the same day?"

"Yes."

"Why do you think she made the inspection at night?"

"She said that she wanted nobody to see her."

"She said it in those terms?"

"Or in similar terms, yes."

"Did you accompany Miss Dickinson on this visual inspection of the land?"

"I would have done so with pleasure, but I was not invited. In any respect, I could quite clearly see Miss Dickinson at the outskirts of our property through my study window, before she came over to our house."

"In the darkness? Even by the light of the moon it appears to me difficult to see a person from so far away...'

David reddened phlegmatically.

"Sir, I am an astronomer. In my house there are many

telescopes, binoculars, every type of instrument designed to see across distances."

"So you remember having seen Miss Dickinson through a telescope or something similar?"

"I repeat: I am an astronomer. I live to observe the world through, as you say, 'a telescope or something similar'." The great majority of times I cannot say whether what I've seen has been with the naked eye or not, I am so used to optical instruments..."

David's sarcastic comment made Mr Taft stumble. He had managed the cross-examination freely, without the theatricality of Hammond, but he had certainly achieved what he wanted. However, if all he needed was to corroborate the testimony of Mabel, that of David Todd was essentially useless.

"I understand. I understand," he said softly.

And he was on the point of asking him to return to his seat when he realized that he still had one more question, which Todd's wife had not known or not wanted to answer.

"Mr Todd, one final question. Could you tell us the value, in money or something similar, of what you paid Mr Dickinson for the house and land in which you currently reside?"

The ironic smile, so recently come to David's face, changed into a sterner, more impenetrable expression. He briefly looked at Mabel, as if searching for something, but she made no motion of response. Hamlin also observed him without being able to disguise the fact that the question was utterly unexpected and that he likewise had no answer.

"Nothing," he replied.

"Say again."

David cleared his throat nervously, and his voice broke into a higher tone than usual.

"I paid nothing for the property. It was a gift of Mr Dickinson, a gift for my wife... and for me."

A medley of exclamations of surprise could clearly be heard around the courtroom. Hamlin turned rapidly to Mabel, his lips suddenly tight in a harsh grimace. The discreet whispers turned to general murmur until Judge Hopkins, with a blow of his gavel on the desk, demanded silence, and ordered David Todd to step down from the witness box.

Before closing the session it was agreed by the defence counsel that Mr Spaulding, of Northampton, would be the next witness.

VII

HAMMOND-TODD

I remained in the refreshment room for the whole interval, walking uneasily from one corner to the other like a caged animal. When the questioning began again I could no longer bear the tension, and collapsed into one of the armchairs without strength to face the testimony of Mr Spaulding. For he knew, he knew full well the reality of what had happened. I could lie to everyone, I could bury Mabel, I could lie to myself, *I had a right to*, but Spaulding was, as far as I could see, a man of good faith, and he didn't deserve to have his credibility tarnished by an affair that he was not even really involved in. I told Hammond and Taft that I felt too weak to attend the hearing, that I would come through later on. Ned went in with them.

In the company of that solemn furniture whose upholstery was striped by time and waiting, I spent my time making a detailed list of all the damage that I had caused around me by my obstinate desire to publish the work of Emily, when she herself had all along rejected the idea. Firstly, the Emilie that I had known, she who lived in the inaccessible garden of her own world, as distant from disputes as she was from both fame and the need of approval. I'll never know if I have not in reality done the most damage to her. Secondly, my brother's family – Sue, Mattie, Ned – could well have been spared the confrontation with that woman. Austin doesn't count, he did enough damage to himself without the help of others. Thirdly, the unwitting accomplices to my lies, starting with poor Mr Spaulding, witness to no more than my desperation; Mr Hill, who will never again want anything to do with me, and who, thank heavens, had decided not to testify; Maggie, worn down by secrets and by that crucial deposition that hung over our heads like a sword; and Reverend Jenkins. And I, although I deserve it, never wished for such humiliation. I am sixty five years old, too little time in front of me to waste in suffering. I have already put my soul in debt, but even so it is in this life, here on earth, where I am paying the debts. And it is this life that counts.

An hour later Ned and Mr Taft appeared with an optimistic, almost exultant expression.

"Spaulding said nothing," was Ned's unexpected announcement.

Taft, calmer, explained to me that Mr Spaulding had not been able to guarantee that I had been fully aware of the content of the document. Moreover, although Taft gave me few details, he suggested that the man had read Maggie's deposition, and that from then on he had wanted to wash his hands of the whole sordid affair as quickly as possible.

But, said the lawyer, even without the support of Spaulding, Judge Hopkins could very well consider the land transfer as legitimate retribution for the work that Mabel undertook. Hamlin, in his first address, had carefully drawn attention to the "profound admiration and love" in the personal relationship between Mabel and Emily, which would certainly lead the Judge to resolve that the Dickinsons had a certain moral and economic obligation towards the Todds, in light of Mabel's work on the poetry. There was just one card still left to play: demonstrate that the bonds between Mabel Todd and Emily Dickinson had been a farce. For me, this involved far more that simply disrespecting Mabel; it was a secret revenge against all those today who, protected by half-truths and the fallibility of memory, claimed to have known my sister so intimately.

When Ned and I returned to the courtroom, Mabel had already been in the witness box for more than twenty minutes. Fortunately for us, Mr Hammond was to be the one to close the examinations, before both lawyers present-ed their summaries.

"You have related with great emotion the most important aspects of your relationship with the deceased, Miss Emily Dickinson," announced Mr Hammond. "Mrs Todd, might we assume therefore that you knew her very well?"

Mabel hesitated. Through the sudden movement of her head searching for the eyes of the lawyer Hamlin, she must have realized at once the ultimate objective of the question. But Hamlin could no longer do anything for her. Finally she replied, smiling broadly, with, as Hammond himself would later recognize, a singular astuteness.

"But of course. Believe me that there is no better way to know a poet than through her work, and God knows I am one of the few people who knows her work so deeply."

"What you mean by that," insisted the lawyer, "is that you knew the deceased, Emily Dickinson of Amherst, ex-clusively through the medium of her work?"

Once again she hesitated in replying: Mabel was trapped. Hammond took advantage of the delay to repeat the question with a tone of voice feigning surprise.

"Mrs Todd: did you know Emily Dickinson personally? In other words, might we assume, for example, that you regularly saw her and spoke to her?"

Mabel turned to her husband, then to me, then to Ned.

"No," she replied.

"You did not regularly see her?"

"I did not."

"Allow me to clarify this point, Mrs Todd. From the first time that you entered the Dickinson house until the time of Miss Emily's death, a period of four and a half years, how many times did you see, speak or participate in gatherings with Miss Emily Dickinson?"

"Never."

"You are saying, therefore, that in over four years you did not see her once? You have brought up several times in this hearing your personal relationship with Miss Dickinson, how can that be?"

"Nobody ever saw Emily Dickinson," said Mabel drily.

I looked at Ned in such a meaningful way that the poor lad, overcome by my expression that he knew so well from my secret imitations of the Reverend, laughed out loud. I, bound to my role of witness, allowed myself no more than a grin, a little disdainful towards Mabel.

"To be frank, it does not appear that the members of the family here present share that view, Mrs Todd..."

And with this perfect irony Hammond, smiling with satisfaction, ended the last of his cross-examinations.

VIII

Ned appeared at the kitchen door this morning, triumphantly brandishing the newspaper in one hand and a bunch of wild bellflowers in the other. Apparently the ruling of Judge Hopkins, although brief, has been published. The court ruled not only that the deed of land transfer has been annulled, that Mabel and David must forfeit the land back to me, but, moreover, that they must pay the legal costs of the suit. It does not surprise me, although a verdict that favours me to such an extent, with diametrically contrary testimonies, would certainly surprise many. Spaulding, the only one who could have tipped the balance against me, in essence said the truth, but the doubt in his words was too transparent. I don't want to think that I have confused him with my lies, rather that none of the facts was ever clear to him from the start – as if they ever were for me, for that matter – and that memory always deceives... On the other hand, it is quite true that Maggie's deposition, behind the scenes, has worked marvels.

I hope that Mabel and David have the decency to send the deed through a third party, and not come here in person. As far as I'm concerned, I wouldn't even permit them to walk past the house.

I have found out, however, that even now I cannot be happy.

It is curious, I scarcely even feel relieved that this nightmare is over. I committed the gravest of sins – I swore a false oath – and the worst thing about this is that I am not the only one who knows. I'm not concerned about Mabel, nor David, nor even Spaulding: I now feel that God and my conscience are my judges, they are what I really fear.

I have started looking at the sky again like when I was a child and I used to steal cookies from the jar that Mother kept in the basement for visitors, with that same sense of panic that would paralyse me on the dark stairway as I fled, hiding the proof of my sin beneath my dress. Suddenly that cookie would change into something sinister, some unbearable weight that would compel me to sit down to try to calm my beating heart. But no, in the darkness of my sin nothing could be calmed, quite the contrary, and I would hear even clearer Mother's footsteps above my head in the kitchen, and I would hear her ordering Emily to fetch the cookie jar *and to count them carefully*; and then I could do nothing more than crush the cookie in my hands and throw the crumbs through the gaps between the stairs. Those nights I could never sleep, imagining that there were, in some corner of the basement, crumbs that would betray me and that God and His army of warrior angels would come during my sleep and suffocate me. That childish certainty that I had of punishment, that my sin would always be discovered, is the same that I feel now, just as childish and irrational. But just as powerful.

I fear God's punishment because my repentance is not sincere, and neither will it ever be. I fear God's punishment because I am incapable of forgiving, because I have perhaps committed the most blundering of all sins in publishing my sister's work: the sin of ambition. And thanks to that sin I have hurt too many people.

IX

God's verdict has taken scarcely two weeks longer to arrive than that of Judge Hopkins, and it will likewise appear in the newspaper, but nobody will perceive it as a punishment but as one more misfortune. Ned, my darling Ned, my sunshine, has just died. This afternoon, barely an hour ago. His heart, the fragile Dickinson heart, suddenly gave out.

I pray only that this heart that I bear within my breast is not the exception.

14

For Parting, That Is Night

For parting, that is night,
And presence, simply dawn –
Itself, the purple on the height
Denominated morn.
                                    – E. Dickinson

*I*t is still winter. It is February and the garden is in darkness – in the shadows, more like – of the trees that still grow, that still try to bind themselves to the earth with all they have, yet remain stunted and hardened by the implacable dryness of the air. And it is cold, the cold of the desert beneath the open sky. I look at the little trees through the library window, the weakened boughs, the twisted knots in the numbed bark. I look at them and take pity on them, thinking that they will never be great and leafy. The blood of the earth freezes them from within. They grow already rotten. No miracles here.

I take pity on myself, that's true, but only on my still-breathing body.

Old Miss Dickinson has reached sixty-six years of age, that's what they'll be saying today in town. They'll say that she's not been able to go to Susan's house, neither has she been able to mend the dress that Mattie asked her for her journey. She has remained in the parlour stroking the keys of the piano, although everyone knows that she cannot play it. She cannot play the piano, and can scarcely even write

257

in her notebook. Pain is like a pair of pliers that twists back one's fingers, one's knees, one's back. When pain comes it is like winter: there is nothing else, nothing else outside, inside, in every hidden corner – there is nothing other than pain. Painkillers are mere drops of water, like lighting a candle in the street, like wanting to warm one of those trees in winter with a candle. Yes, they are no more than the weak flame of a candle to warm a winter tree...

However, it is good here at home, here in front of the warm fire with this woollen rug over my skirt. Maggie is baking gingerbread in the kitchen, and the heavy scent of spices wafts through the rooms just as when Emilie used to make her pies and tarts. Sixty-six years old! Mattie says that age is nothing, that nowadays, almost at the turn of the twentieth century, modern medicine will help people live to a hundred years without a problem. Could there be anybody, I wonder, who would honestly want to live a hundred years? Perhaps in the future world they'll find the way to prevent memory becoming a burden, to prevent all one's memories weighing as much as one's own bones, deforming them like my arthritic fingers are deformed every morning. Maybe the world to come will be different, that's true, but I do not belong there, neither do I belong in this one, nor the world where Emilie and Austin trod, nor that of Father and Mother, nor even Joseph's – I do not belong in that world in which this house was the house of the Dickinsons, and was the only brick house in the town.

Today, I suspect, the children play their games imagining that this is an abandoned castle, where an old witch lives surrounded by cats, forever combing her long black hair that reaches to her waist with her knotty fingers that resemble withered branches, all beneath the gentle protection of those old trees.

Last night something wonderful happened: I had that dream again that predicts the forthcoming sweet relief of death.

This time, the machine of black cogs was within my breast. I could see it from outside, as if I could see myself from outside of myself, seated at the foot of my bed. The regular creaking of the empty rocking chair beside the bed, the dirty light that filtered through the closed windows – all these details were familiar to me. Father was spying through the crack in the door, Mother was laughing somewhere off in the distance, where she couldn't be seen. Mother was laughing? Perhaps she was feeling happy, like when she listened to the Jenny Lind concert. Why was Father spying without daring to enter? Why was Emilie not in the rocking chair, waiting for me, and why wasn't Austin insisting on the chloroform? No, it wasn't the same dream at all. Stuck in this wretched variant I tried in vain to wake myself up. Suddenly the door of the room opened and from the threshold, with his tired little face, Gilbert held out his arms to me. Gilbert! I stretched out all I could from the bed, the cogs within me began to turn and loose their mesh and the wheels span wildly, grinding as if my breast were the sound chamber of some monstrous instrument, grumbling and halting, advancing and breaking. But I did not care because Gil was at the door with his little hands opened, ready to take my hands in his.

Then, as if swept away by a sudden wind, the little fellow disappeared. Gilbert, the room, the rocking chair, the light. Everything. Gone.

In the semi-darkness of my room other eyes gazed at me with an impassive glow. It was old Drummy, my most beloved pussy cat, purring on my chest. Had he perhaps scared away the ghost of his old pursuer? Who had scared whom?

Cats, I have been sure for some time, can look after themselves in the face of spectres. They do not weary themselves in fighting useless battles, like excited dogs winding themselves up barking at them; on the contrary, cats treat the spirits with disdain, in an offhand manner, indifferent – essentially a code of coexistence. Aside from spectres there is nothing more remote than the thoughts of a cat: both substances drift in the same type of atmosphere. That is why I live surrounded by my pussy cats: they are my intermediaries, the voices of what I cannot see during my waking hours.

I look through the southern windows at the hills of Pelham. They knew how to be blue, is that not true, Maggie? There is no longer any landscape since Ned died. Maybe the land-scape *is* there, yet I can no longer see it. This court case has taken away my desire to live, and yet I feel that I have fulfilled my duty. You, Maggie, are the one who says that the fulfilling of a duty has more value than anything else. I have done it, much to my regret, and you know it to be true.

What will you do when I am no longer here, Maggie? Will you take good care of my dear pussy cats? Will you ensure that nobody, except Mattie, lives in this house?

Some people say that the world will end soon, that God will send a storm of stars to finish everything. I am tempt-ed to believe that I will disappear before something of that nature occurs, and that in any respect, it is no more than the unfounded fear of those who still have something remaining of their lives. What will one more number mean to God, one century or another, one life more or less, one planet more or less in the universe?

I have spoken at length with Mattie about the future. She did not want to; and even today, seeing me almost immobile through the pain of my bones, she refuses to think about my death, and happily says that there are still Dickinsons left for me to bury. I spoke to her in any respect, overcoming both her fear and mine, which for me is no longer the fear of death nor the end of the world, but the fear that my final wishes will not be respected as I have respected the wishes of those who came before me, without questioning. I assured her that I will turn into her guardian angel, and, should it ever be necessary, into her avenging angel. "Aunt Vinnie, the eternal zealot," Mattie said with her customary sweetness. But I know that she has taken to heart the things I said.

I made her promise me two things.

The first is that she will burn all the correspondence that belongs to me, regardless of whether I have written it myself or received and filed it. I asked her not to give in to pain, solitude, nor that covetousness which arises from the need to keep close those whom we have loved. Nothing – I don't want to leave behind me one single miserable scrap of paper. I have done it for others, burning the letters of Joseph Lyman, of Mother, of Father. If I kept from the flames Emilie's papers it was because they did not belong to me, but to the world. The world will burn them in its own way, or not, who can say today? From the precise moment in which I found them in her room I knew that I didn't have it within me to destroy them, and that is why I do not feel it to be a betrayal of her will.

The second has to do with the battle of my final years, a personal battle that has stained this chapter of my life, although I fear that she will find it difficult to carry out. I made Mattie promise that she will erase the name of Mabel Todd from the books of Emilie. Until that happens, neither my body below nor my soul on earth will be able to rest, if, indeed, after all this I deserve any rest.

And I have one final favour to ask you, Maggie, which is also a plea. I have hidden in a chest, under lock and key, some of Emily's letters and all the poems that I've managed to rescue from Mabel, also from Sue, and all those poems that for my part I've been discovering over the course of these years in the backs of drawers or folded up in bits of paper. There are love letters and short little poems written in the hand of her final years, so erratic and diffuse that they are hard to read. I greatly fear that most of them had been rejected for being too anarchic in their rhyme, perhaps even by Emily herself, or because nobody ever attempted to decipher them. None of this matters now, Maggie, only that those poems and letters have been kept, and it is in secret that I entrust you with revealing them or not, in the appropriate moment.

You'll ask why I have asked this of you and not of Sue or Mattie. To be honest with you, since Ned died I cannot trust even my own shadow. And I wouldn't have even left this secret with Ned. I have fought so hard to see the work of Emily published, that now, the closest I have ever been to death, I even doubt whether my honest intentions have actually been any more or less selfish than those of that woman. However I am certain of something: all that I have managed to have published up to now shows the only Emily possible. This fact cannot be changed, nobody can undo it, Maggie, and you cannot imagine how much and how often I feel the weight of it. For the whole world, Emily Dickinson is and always will be a myth, a fantastic genius, captive in an interminable succession of prisons: that of her gypsy looks, of her white clothing, of that sterile daguerreotype when she was seventeen, the prison of failed love and the prison of chastity, and finally, the prison of the walls of this house.

That chrysalis is Emily Dickinson to the eyes of the world, and that is how she will continue to be. My sister, however, is in reality on those papers that I've just mentioned to you.

Yes, I was able to modify her appearance in a photograph, to transform her pulled-back hair into careless curls, to add that mother-of-pearl cameo or to soften the starched austerity of her collar, but I could never transform her voice. What is written is her, and she is what is written – *everything* that she has written, and also this voice. As I said before, I now even doubt my own intentions, and now I cannot even determine whether what I have done has turned out well, or at least favourably, for Emilie. The Belle of Amherst will perhaps thank me one day, so, perhaps, will those who survived her and now cash in on some undeserved or inherited fame. But my sister? What did I do with her reluctance to publish her poems? *Publication – is the Auction of the Mind of Man.* She wrote that. And what have *I* done, Maggie, with her imperious need for privacy, her final years in the kitchen making bread and cakes, with her plans to marry and be a woman with a husband, and her flea-ridden dog and distant nieces and nephews, and her spinster sister, wilted and alone?

I wonder what I have done with my sister – Good Lord I wonder, Maggie, where, in which act of selfishness and insolence I have lost her.

I cannot avoid thinking that I am a monster, and that I have created another monster on my path to oblivion. For no one will know anything about me – my happiness and my sorrow will come holding hands with that same ghost until I breathe my last.

What I have left you is more a duty than an entreaty, Maggie, don't think I'm not fully aware of that. I ask you beyond anything else to forgive me. I don't know what to do. I feel that whichever step I take will be a false one, that defending what I've done will betray me, and that hiding what I've already hidden is betraying her.

Can you understand what I'm saying?

Could anyone understand it?

Sue, for example. What would she have done in my position? She more than anyone wanted to save Emilie from harsh criticism, and she would rather have kept her hidden than expose the misery of her own family, the dishonour of Austin and Mabel that would have fuelled gossip like a twisted form of vengeance. Had it been up to her, the ashes of those papers would have enriched the air a long time ago. Or Mattie – what could she have done, if the decisions of life seem only to consume her every moment of the day? Friends of earlier years whom I could have turned to for advice, like Sam Bowles, Reverend Wadsworth, dear Helen, or even Joseph Lyman – they are all gone. The only survivors are enemies, who would not think twice about pouncing like voracious rats upon each and every word, reducing Emily's writings to the same filth that soils their lives.

Will you know what to do with them, my dear, faithful Maggie?

I remember the first time that we went to clean Emilie's room, after the funeral; nothing, neither plea nor threat, would induce you to accompany me. I remember that you said to me: "Miss Emily will suffer." So many years later I must now admit that you were right, in fact you were doubly right – we've all suffered. I cannot help thinking that my sister left a large part of her poems in the trunks in your room, and that in doing so, unexpected as such an act may appear to everyone, even to me, Emilie had her own clear reasons that I was unable to understand at the time. I don't want to make the same mistake twice, Maggie. Your heart is wise, noble, unsullied by pain or ambition – believe me that I know it will guide you well. If only I could trust in my own heart in the same way, but the Dickinson heart is fragile, and mine scarcely even beats enough to keep me alive.

In any respect it is the world around me that has now finally stopped and not my heart. I breathe an air that is not from here, the same musty amber air that the portraits and ancient armchairs of this house breathe. Not the violet of the sunset, nor the rich black of the forest, nor the blue of the mountains, nor the friendly gravestones. None of this belongs to me. The whole century melts away before my eyes. Is it not clear that these eyes can no longer cry, that they will most likely not see the spring?

However it is not dying that scares me, rather what will come after. Beyond everything else the fear of death is no more than the fear of letting go of something that you've loved or possessed in some way, and believe me I share nothing of that sentiment. The people I loved are spirits who dance in the garden. The objects I've owned have lost their form since my hands lost the ability to hold them. Nothing I leave has enough value or weight to cause me any suffering or loss. That is not a great consolation, but at least I know that I am going to cross the threshold of death without holding back, as light as the dry leaves of the holm oak that flutter up and away with the wind, never to return...

Epilogue

*L*avinia Norcross Dickinson died on 31st August 1899. They say that throughout her last days she repeated over and over again, "Remove that woman's name from my sister's book."

After the funeral Maggie left the house, and her whereabouts were never known. Negligence, coupled with forgetfulness, certainly did not help to find her.

After the lawsuit, Mabel Loomis Todd did not take up again her conferences on the poetry of Emily Dickinson. In 1917 the couple moved to Florida, and in 1922 David Todd was admitted to the first of what would be many psychiatric institutions, in which, until the day of his death, he worked on a complex engineering system to discover eternal life.

Mabel died in 1932 of a brain haemorrhage, and since then her daughter, Millicent Todd Bingham, began to publish both the manuscripts of Emily Dickinson that had remained with her mother, and her own memories of the history of the Dickinsons. It is worth clarifying that references to the participation of Lavinia Dickinson in the life and work of her sister Emily are diametrically opposed in the memoirs of Martha Dickinson Bianchi and Millicent Todd Bingham.

Martha Dickinson Bianchi, "Mattie", was the last surviving member of the Dickinson family. The house of her aunts and grandparents passed into ownership of Amherst College, and is today the Emily Dickinson Museum. The house of her parents, more commonly known as the Evergreens, is not usually open to the public, but thanks to a series of legal manoeuvres it remains unchanged, preserved exactly as it was at the beginning of the century, even against the final and expressed wish of Martha: that once the last occupant of the house died, the Evergreens should be demolished, down to the foundations.